A] Chemi...

by

F.E. Birch

For Karen

My dearest friend

Bowl of Cherries

In 1974 I was twelve, a big boy for my age, and I was shipped off to Aunty Jenny for the summer. I learnt an awful lot that year. Actually, it wasn't all that awful.

Creatures like Aunt Jenny didn't exist in our quiet corner of Northumberland. She was colourful and brash, and my father always said the further away she was from him the better he felt. Some bitter family history was all I knew. I guess he just didn't like her. The only thing he did like about her was that she was living so far away. However, he wasn't averse to sending me to her and I never understood that.

The large beautiful house in Hampshire, bequeathed to her when Uncle Jimmy died, was as vibrant and bounteous in its furnishings as she was. Abundant and fertile foliage sheltered hidden secrets within the widespread boundaries of the house. Magnificent mysteries were mine to uncover, the magnitude of which I misinterpreted with the ignorance of boyish eagerness.

And then I had the first exploration, the first discovery, the realisation; that first footstep into an awakening, sexual world.

WE WERE TRYING to hide from the hot pelting rain when she took me by the hand and led me to her den, the place she called her play-palace. It was hidden in the depths of her lush orchard, with rich, ripe cherries dangling down, ready and ripe for picking. Inside the play-palace the fragrance was as arresting as she was, aromas of soft fruit and fanciful perfumes. It seemed a miraculous discovery and I loved it. I let my fingers trail patterns in the silks and stockings that were hanging on the low clothing rail beneath the rammed bookshelf. I blushed rich red as I saw naked ladies and proud men in the magazines she had on display.

Jenny lit a joss stick and pushed it into the core of a shiny green apple perched next to the overflowing ashtray on her dressing table. Ladies' things covered every surface and I took in the rich cacophony of colour; purple, pink, and red lipsticks, peachy powders, rainbow shades of nail varnish and thick black pencils for eyes. I loved the fat, soft-bristled brushes that invited me to run a finger through them. I smoothed my hand over the top of the largest, imagining a purring kitten responding to my touch. I watched it sprung forward and back again in slow motion and I was enrapt with a fleeing image of a bird taking flight, up and away. I did it again and her low guttural laugh sent a shiver down my back as she came and stood behind me.

'Come … sit with me.' Her light smoky breath brushed the top of my ear.

Tingling spread down my spine and to my groin as I experienced hitherto unknown feelings.

She walked to the corner of the room and she sat herself down on the futon bed, falling into the suede patchwork covering. She crossed her long, smooth legs, and leant back. She patted the space beside her and fell against plump pillows.

'Rodney…come here…I don't bite.'

She smiled her red plush lips and I watched as a flash of wet tongue traced them. She crooked a long fingernail at me.

'Come on,' she purred, patting the patchwork again.

I looked at the floor, my face burning, and tried to scuff my toes into the joins between the polished wooden floorboards. I dug my hands deep into the pockets of my jeans that were suddenly too small, my face hot as the raindrops we'd tried to avoid evaporated with the heat of the room.

'Roddy…come to me,' she ordered, sharper this time.

I walked, propelled towards her. I couldn't help it. I sat down, clasped my hands between my knees and crossed my ankles. I shivered as her finger stroked my cheek. It felt as light as a snowdrop, as tickly as a feather. The room was so hot, yet a chill ran down my back.

She scooped her arm into the bend of mine and I relaxed a little, waiting for her next move. She talked to me like she liked me, like my father never did. She asked all about me, what I enjoyed doing, what I didn't. She made me miss my mum, even though I'd never known her. Once she'd discovered everything I had to tell, she encouraged me to discover all about her. And I did. Every day for three weeks.

Sometimes, as I lay in my bed, laughter rippled through the moonlight into the open attic window. Light music danced into my room, wafting with the musky smells that came from her palace. I hugged myself tight and imagined being there with her, as I remembered the soft touch of her flesh, the smoothness of her skin, the curve of her waist and the bulge of her breast. I shivered at the memory of the lady parts she wanted me to kiss, lick, and enjoy. I fell asleep to images of her and her fingers light and playful as she tickled my back, the only thing that she'd ever done to touch me, despite my pleading for more.

When it was time to leave, to go back to sleepy Northumberland, she kissed me full on the lips as her housekeeper prepared the car to take me to the station. Then she laughed, and said, 'Come back next year to sample the delights of Eros.'

BY 1977, IT was different. I had been a boy but now I was a man and I had enough seed to scatter the whole of the orchard. She hadn't sent for me as usual, and I didn't understand. This was the year that I could prove myself to her and she was irresistible to me. I persuaded my father to talk to his sister. He compromised his principles by asking her for something, and he'd managed to talk her into two weeks during August. I had instructions from my father to do exactly what she said and if I didn't, I'd be straight home. I promised I would do anything she wanted. He didn't realise what he was saying didn't and I didn't realise exactly what she had in mind.

PERHAPS I WAS too demanding, too eager to indulge. I lay on the familiar bed in the attic, looking up at the glow-in-the dark ceiling stars she'd given me to remind me of her back on that first trip. Bright stars, shooting rockets, full moons all sparkled at me and that first day filtered into view – the hot, rainy day when she'd introduced me to the forbidden pleasures of Eve, to the naughty secretive places a young boy couldn't imagine existed when he was twelve.

This time I'd brought her gifts; red silk lingerie, shoplifted from the store in town, plush silk roses, and soft musk joss sticks. I'd also brought her some hash as a special gift. I smiled, listening to the soft tweeting of the birds in the branches where the sun fell, dappling down into the summer lane. I breathed in the heady, succulent air. I was hot, sweaty, and full of randy anticipation.

I swept myself from bed on the first day of August. The housekeeper told me Aunt Jenny was in the garden. She was waiting for me!

I hurried to our den, following the wafting welcoming incense as it mixed with the sweet and rich cloying cherries of the orchard. I detected an undercurrent of weed. Soft music tinkled louder as I approached, an instrumental piece by Vangelis. I was all but bursting out of my trousers when I reached the den and pushed the door ajar.

She sat up in an instant, naked, making no attempt to try to cover herself. Her breasts jangled against the curly head of a bare dusky-coloured boy who looked far younger than me. He looked up from his kneeling position, his wet mouth grinning at me. She was smiling and asked me to join them, stoned and full of sex.

'Come, Roddy, show him what you have learnt, you're my star pupil.' She leant forward, full lips pouting.

I unfastened my Chinos and dropped them to the floor. My underwear fell and I kicked my clothes away as I took stock of the sight before me.

'My, oh my.' She grinned. 'How you've grown.'

She wiped her lips on the white tissues and left a red streak, like blood, like my soul.

'I've taught you well, Roddy. You can go now. Out into the wide world. Shut the door as you leave, I'm rather busy.'

I stared at her. It was a moment too long. 'I thought I could show your friend here how to do it properly before I left,' I said. 'I could give him a lesson on female anatomy, show him how it works…if you like.'

I could see her mulling it over as she looked from me to him. He sat on the floor, like a puppy wanting more, nodding at her, eyes wide and glistening with the effects of cannabis and cunnilingus that hung stagnant in the air.

Skinning up, I took a chance. 'As I'm here, you might as well make the best of me.' Licking the Rizla paper, I stared at her, intense eyeball to eyeball. Lighting the reefer, I flopped onto the bed beside her and stroked her left breast. Her nipple was dark red, like one of the succulent cherries that hung in her orchard. She leant back, melting into my hands, her eyes closing.

'Why not…' she murmured, fingering the tight reefer from me. She took a long drag.

I told him to sit on the wooden chair and watch. I slid the bolt across the inside of the den door. I picked a selection of the darkest red scarves from the hangers. I tied her ankles to the bed posts and then did the same to her wrists, tying them above her head.

'What do you think, Cory Boy?' I had no idea what his name was, but Cory seemed to suit him. Especially for what I had in mind.

He nodded his curls up and down and I could see he was gagging. I positioned him on a chair at the end of the bed, facing her splayed legs. I tied his hands around the back of the wooden frame.

'Roddy…I hope you're not hurting him,' Jenny said, lifting her head to look.

'I'm teaching him, Aunt Jenny, like you taught me. Remember when you asked me to tie you like this? Remember when you taught me how to explore? Well, Cory has a ringside seat, no extra charge.'

She laughed. 'And I thought you'd be angry with me, Rodney. Seems like I underestimated you.'

'I think perhaps you did.' I smiled as I picked up an apple from the bowl piled high with fresh fruit. I peeled it with the small knife she used for just that purpose. I let the skin curl round and drop onto her body. I sliced the apple into long thin pieces and fed them to her, then to him, and ate the last sharp slice myself. I ran my index finger along the top of the blade and contemplated what I was about to do.

Once I'd started, I couldn't stop. I remembered every time she'd taken me to heaven, and then to hell, and the passion rose. As Vangelis played out, I stabbed and stabbed inside her, oblivious to the screaming orgasm. I penetrated her like never before, finishing with the finale. The paring knife sliced deep inside, and then I cut out the biggest cherry of all. Holding it tight, I moved up to her face and slit her mouth like a clown. She wore a permanent smile, rendering her face asunder.

Cory Boy, my alibi, my motive; I slit his mouth too, but I didn't want him to die. She'd been the sacrifice; he was the witness.

I ran naked through the orchard, screeching like a squaw. I smeared their mingled blood in tribal warrior style across my chest, across my cheeks. Whooping and wailing, I collapsed in a bundle of ragged nerves and shredded emotion in the middle of the trees.

And the rich ripe cherries tumbled…and fell…and kept falling…all the rotten fruit from the tree.

All About Joanna

I was six the first time I saw a dead body. I don't remember it, but I know I saw it. Her. Joanna. The girl who was my best friend. Who was dead.

I know how old I was because Mam had a baby in her tummy. My sister was born just before my seventh birthday and she wasn't there yet so I know I must have been six.

Once my sister was born, and after the bad thing happened, we moved to a different place. I went to a different school, made different friends, and I gradually forgot all about Joanna.

Everything changed after the move and I hated it. Sometimes Aunty Marge would come and take me to stay with her for a few days. We'd take her yappy little dog for walks up to the park and through the cemetery. When I was eight, Aunty Marge showed me a grave.

'It's really sad when young people die,' she said. 'Do you remember her?'

'Who?' I asked.

'Joanna?'

I saw the name on the white headstone – Joanna Harvey, died tragically, aged seven.

Joanna. I felt a pain, sharp like a dart from the dartboard Aunty Marge's husband had. I was hit by sad, a big cloud of it, and I felt something like a big black spider crawling into my belly, rummaging around inside, chewing at me, making a big black hole. A lump grew in my throat, which was instantly dry. I couldn't speak.

Then I saw her, Joanna. She stood there, smiling at me, and it was like I had never forgotten her at all.

WHEN I WENT home, there was a terrible row.

'Why would you take a kid to a cemetery?' Mam screamed at Aunty Marge.

'She needs to remember! To deal with it,' Aunty Marge screamed back.

'No, she doesn't. She needs to forget. And she had. She'd forgotten all about it!'

'She needs to grieve. Her best friend died. And she saw it happen!'

I didn't see Aunty Marge for many years after that.

Joanna. She had lovely long blonde hair and bright blue eyes that smiled when her mouth did. She was very pretty. She was in Mrs Thomas's class and she was seven. I was in Mrs Frith's class and I was six and looked up to her. There was a big difference between being six and being seven.

Ashley, her brother, was four. He followed us around like a little puppy dog, his little tongue hanging out, his brown eyes sparky and bright. He was a cheeky boy and a pesky pest. He was also cute.

All the kids played in the back streets and we weren't allowed to play around the front because our Mam's said it was dangerous when cars and trucks trundled past. Ashley didn't understand. One day he ran around the front. Joanna ran after him and I ran after her. Ashley laughed; thought we were chasing him. He looked back at us, laughing. He ran into the road.

Joanna pushed him out of the way. She saved her brother's life.

I saw it because I was there, but like young children do, I forgot the bad thing that happened because it was so very bad. Sometimes I remembered fragments and caught a glimpse of Joanna smiling, but I quickly forget again. Sometimes I heard the screaming. But I've never remembered the car that hit her, or what happened next.

Now she's back. Joanna. She stands above my bed and smiles with eyes that smile with her mouth. She makes sure I'll never forget her again.

Hot in the City

Celia hated summer. She was sticky. Sex did that to a girl in the summer.

The Police Chief succumbed to the Rohypnol as she slipped the syringe into his eye duct. It was a squeeze and when it was done, she departed the seedy Soho bedsit, stepped out from the dark hallway, and into the sweltering city. She smiled as she thought about the three wise monkeys.

Bright sunlight hit her with a dazzle and her enthusiasm mounted apace with all the excitement and fervour of those who pounded her skinny body. She patted her purse as it hung by a silver thread over her shoulder. She looked up to the sky and it was as blue as lips on the Chief. Celia was clever. She smiled as she traced a manicured fingertip along the outline of the hypodermic needle hidden in her bag. She'd need a refill before the next one.

Celia's sparkling heels clattered out of tune as she strode along the gum-spattered pavement of the tired West End. Her hair was up, she was hot, in need of a drink and time to think. Beads of sweat turned into rivulets down her back like melting snow, but not as chilled. It was hot enough to curdle milk. Halter-necks and short skirts made no difference on a day like this, which is why she'd left her bra dangling down from his neck. She didn't need it and it looked so pert and pretty wrapped around his windpipe.

CELIA LOOKED AT the watch hanging loosely from her wrist. A present from a john, encrusted with fake diamonds and all about the bling. Five minutes before twelve. The clip-joints had started to play boom-boom music. Too loud, it reverberated in the street, bouncing off high buildings. Girls were coming to life. Traffic belched unhealthy fumes. The air was still and she had a few hours to kill. The Saveloy Bar would soon be open. She'd take refuge there, no questions asked. And she'd pick up a tote or two for later. Tommo owed her for a favour done last Sunday when he was gagging.

She turned from Wardour Street into the heart of sleaze. The place was filling up like a boil. Celia leant against a wall to light a cigarillo. She brought up her right knee, foot against the pebbledash that insisted on prickling her pert behind. A quick flash of sweaty toffee-coloured thigh and white crotch-less panties was good for business. She flicked a flame to life and let it dance while she rummaged for her pack of six. Celia liked to tease, especially in summer. It was all about confidence.

It was easy, as most men were. It didn't take much. Men of Power were game boys. They liked to act tough, but she had them melting in her hand. Miss Vanilla Ice. She exhaled, one smoke ring at a time. One down. Two left. The judge. And the barrister. Both lifetime friends of her adopted father. The first three men to screw her. It was her turn now. And she was gagging for it.

Boy, was she hot.

Look Me in the Eye

It might have been because he'd seen me naked, when was spying on me through the keyhole on the bathroom door. It might have been because he was screwed in the head. It might have been because he just felt like it, at that time, on that day, with me.

But he's dead now and nobody will ever know for sure.

Maybe you, my jury, you won't believe me. I can only tell you my story as it is, as I see it, and hope that what I say moves you enough to take my word against that of a dead body, a keen pathologist's report, and a slick prosecution team. Of course, it's their job to make you sure, sure beyond all reasonable doubt of my guilt. There is only me to tell you otherwise. I have no fancy tricks, no impressive defence team, and no glossy word gymnastics to convince you. I'm already condemned by my conscience. I will never sleep easy again. Whatever you decide, it won't change the facts. I killed a man.

THE CHINK OF water-filled glasses, bulbous and thick, sounded in the courtroom as the public gallery cleared and the jury filed out for a working lunch in the room designated just for them and their deliberations. Katya Shakova leant back in the dock, eyes closed, and sensed the prosecutor was ogling her, his eyes rolling up her legs to the crevice between her bare thighs. She smirked without opening her eyes and leant back against the wooden slats of the dock, resting her arms against the top rail. She crossed her legs. Slowly. She poked her tongue through her rouge-red lips, parting them ever so slightly for desired effect. She heard muted voices, whispers in hairy ears. She heard the shuffling of robes and the scuff of black brogue feet. Then silence.

She cracked open her black mascaraed lashes and saw their eyes, like tiny currants in hot-cross buns, staring at her. She smiled.

WHAT HAPPENED? I know you want to know. I could tell you all about my life, how I was abused by my grandfather, how I was left at seventeen to bring up three younger sisters in poverty. I could tell you how I came to your country destitute, broken, and pimped. That's my history. What more can I say?

I broke the cycle, snapped the chain, and made a life. *How* is not what's important. I found myself in a remote part of Scotland, in a land of tall men who wore skirts, ladies with aprons like my grandma, and countryside littered with dangerous water sports. I was a foreigner with a suitcase full of money and I discovered a beautiful cottage with bobbing begonia's in the back garden, fragrant roses crawling up the front door, and clematis under the windowsills. It was the cottage on the jigsaw box, the shortbread tin feature, that picture postcard you send to your old aunt. I bought it. Cash.

I needed a job. I found one in a little independent book shop nestled behind a tourist attraction waterfall. Part time, of course, because outsiders could only find part time work. I didn't mind. They gave me a discount on books.

I had a spare room, so I looked for a lodger. And that's how I met Romanov. He was thirty-seven, twelve years older than me, and like me, he was an outsider. He said he was passing through, trying to find his way. I knew what he meant because I was too.

He worked in the industrial laundry and his hands were soft, conditioned, and very long, like his face. He played me like a Stradivarius, and we made beautiful music with sexual overtures. I told him I may have loved him, in a different life, if I had been made that way.

One night he suggested a take-away, something Chinese, but our little town didn't have one. We had a fish and chip shop, a pub that made pizza, and a cockroach curry house. He got angry and ranted in his mother tongue. That was the first time I saw his wrath, but I'd known worse in my life, so I ignored it. I cast his mood aside as an occupational hazard of a lover.

I soon learnt he liked to play games. Scrabble. Hide and Seek. And Blind Man's Buff.

Yes, ladies and gents, you heard me correctly. Blind Man's Buff. I wasn't so keen on the kinky stuff, but he liked it that way, menacing and tormenting with that stare of his. I didn't want to go there, to discover that side of him, or me, but I relented after the first few times. Of course, he wanted more.

KATYA ASKED FOR a recess, for time to gather her thoughts, to collect herself and steady the nervous energy jangling through her body, causing a red rush in her ears and red butterflies across her chest.

Ten minutes, Lord Justice Favier agreed.

The jury filed out again, little ants entranced and captivated by the black-haired beauty who was weaving her tale, crafting her defence, and making them fall in love with her.

Katya remained standing as she took a sip of ice-chilled water and let it dribble down the back of her raging throat. The public gallery watched. The prosecution team avoided her eye. The police officers looked uncomfortable from their relegated position with the press. Dramatic pause, the journalist wrote in his scrappy notebook, the air charged with sparks of silver, red, black atoms of anticipation as the courtroom awaited the big reveal.

Katya cleared her throat. She smoothed down her short black skirt and tweaked the collar of her pristine white blouse. She twiddled her gold looped earrings in a circular motion, aware of the attention she was provoking. She played with a mole on her neck, a little bobbling just above her collar bone, off to the right. She read the bundle of court papers. A frown creased her forehead as she slipped the top sheet to the back of the pile and read some more. A delicate cough echoed around the room and she patted her mouth with her hand, fingers deliberate and slender. Silence hovered and everyone waited for her next move like she was playing a cool game of chess.

Katya finally swivelled on her heels and turned to face Judge Favier, who nodded to the usher, a signal for the jury to return. She coughed again, a light tinkle into her hand.

She began.

Romanov was hungry. He wanted food, cooked by me, so we went shopping in our little town, in the supermarket in the square. You have seen CCTV evidence of this produced by the prosecution team. Yes, we bought chicken. And rice. Peppers. Onions. Beer. And vodka, Russian.

And so I cooked. We ate and he said he was going back to his homeland. He said he would bring me back a present. A tattoo.

I laughed. 'How can you bring me back a tattoo?'

'I have it just for you,' he gushed. 'On my ass.'

I laughed some more. He was being funny.

He did not like my humour. He said, 'You laugh at me. Is not nice.'

'Sorry, Roman. I like you. But please. Not my name.' I toyed with him. I admit it. It was for a joke.

He grabbed my wrist. Pulled me forward across the table from where I sat opposite him.

He spat in my face. 'Ouch! You hurt me, Roman.'

'Not like I can hurt you. I can hurt you real bad. You get?'

'Yes. Yes, I get. Please. Let me go.' In that moment I knew I wanted him to go to his motherland and not come back.

He snarled at me. 'I shall tattoo you. On your ass. You are mine now.'

Members of the jury. He tied me to my chair. He took my dressing gown cord and tied me tight where I sat. And then he fed me. He fed me like a baby, all chicken and rice and peppers tumbling down my chin.

After the feast he took a cigar. And he branded me. On my ass. He took his cigar and he branded me, circular and red and now scarred like a penny coin. This, ladies and gentlemen, is my exhibit. My tattoo from Romanov.

It turned him on. Aroused him like a Greek God on display in a tourist hovel. He liked to play games, so after the branding he brought out his toys. Sex toys. You've seen them too, the toys. I watched as you all touched them with your hands and your eyes. You felt them, you know how they feel. Soft. Rubbery. Hard. Mechanical. Smooth. Rough. Joy. And pain. One of you, yes, I saw, one of you, you sniffed them, couldn't help yourself. They are the toys he used and how could I refuse? How could I? Romanov was a man who was used to having what he wanted, and that included me.

When he finished with the toys, he unfastened me from the wooden kitchen chair. He said, 'Dance with me.'

I danced with him. We had made beautiful music, once. But not on this day.

He asked me to tie him to the chair. I did what I had to do. I tied him to the chair. He loved to play games, Romanov. He was persuasive … and violent. Who was I to disagree? He was a man who liked to push boundaries, liked to take it to the limit, loved the thrill.

When he told me to strip, I stripped.

When he told me to take the knife from under my pillow, I knew then he'd always known it was there. I had it for my protection. In my own country I needed to protect myself and my sisters so was used to sleeping with a knife for company. I took it from under my pillow and knew at that moment he would have found my money, too. When I brought him the knife, his eyes spoke to me and told me he knew all about my money.

He asked me to move closer to him so he could smell me. I didn't want him to smell me. I could smell me. It was the fear of a thousand rabbits caught in a bright light. It was the fear of a little girl hiding under the bed from her grandfather. It was the fear of a woman held captive by a dangerous and violent man.

I took a fairy footstep forward. Then another. I held the knife. He watched me and he smiled. He liked games. He told me to put my bra over his face so he could inhale me. I picked it up from the floor where it lay in a squiggle on top of my pile of clothes. I put the knife in his hand, and he held it like a sharp serrated penis. I fastened my 34C bra over his eyes, just how he liked it. I made it a tight fit and he moaned in delight and ecstasy. I could see his erection bobbing beneath his pants.

27

He jumped forward in the chair, a little frog jump across the slate floor. He wobbled, fell forward. He yelled. His big sweaty body was too heavy and too tied to move. I knew the knife must have gone into his big wobbling belly. It must have slipped and slid inside him, a hand into a glove.

I screamed. Romanov bellowed like a bull, a noise like a dinosaur might have made. I ran around the room, screaming, and then I went to him and tried to lift the chair. He was heavy. I moved the chair up an inch … two … three …but he was too strong for me. I couldn't hold him. I couldn't lift any higher and the chair fell. Romanov howled some more, from deep in his chest, just like that dinosaur.

Deep deep red spread across the floor like spilled paint and watched, fascinated, as it grew wider, rounder, redder. What to do?

He moaned. He groaned. He jabbered in Russian and I didn't understand. But I did understand.

Members of the jury, I panicked. I grabbed some clothes from the laundry pile Romanov had brought home from work that day. I dressed. I ran. And I ran. And I ran.

I found a policeman on School Lane. I told him I had killed a man.

He laughed at me.

Jury, I told him I killed a man and he laughed. He then told me to go to the police station and gave me directions because I didn't know where it was. I ran to the police station.

It was closed.

I banged on the door. I shouted again and again, 'I killed a man! I killed a man!' I was desperate. I needed help. Romanov needed help. But nobody came.

I found my way into a bar and asked to use their telephone. It was hanging from the wall and I was sure it wouldn't work. I tapped the little black buttons and I dialled 999. I told the person who answered, 'I killed a man.'

And the rest, I have told.

JURY. LOOK ME in the eye. I feel as guilty of killing a man as if I plunged that knife into his body myself. I tried to help, and I didn't stop running until breath had left my body and my chest was red raw. I didn't pull that knife from Romanov. I panicked. I was scared. He was a wild animal like an extinct dinosaur, and I was scared liked a bewitched rabbit. Yes, he was sometimes a loving beast, but not always. I knew I couldn't not help him. He was too big for me, in every way.

Look me in the eye and if you think I'm guilty of murder, beyond all reasonable doubt, then convict me.

Look me in the eye and if you think I'm not guilty of murder, beyond all reasonable doubt, then you must let me go.

My life in your hands, jury. But hear this.

I will carry the pain of killing a man … forever.

On the Beach

'What time is it?'

Nobody answers.

'Please, what time is it?'

Still no reply.

'I've been here ages, and nobody ever comes.'

She'd hoped that they might have started to look for her by now. It had been such a long time. But it *was* a great hiding place and soon the dark would come.

'It's when I'm most alone, at night-time.' Her light voice carries around in the smoky evening breeze. Many hours have passed and when the sun does shine, it doesn't shine on her.

'I thought Uncle Jack might have come to see I haven't gone away. Maybe he can't find his way back.' A solitary conversation in the chilled night air, a lonely little girl's thoughts that toy with her.

'I'm freezing. It's so cold, I'm very cold, my skin and my bones are icy.' The sun has long gone and the clang of the Steelworks rattle around her as waves crash onto the wide empty beach.

Still nobody listens and when the noises stop, she continues to hear the echoes in the chill night air.

'GO AND PLAY Jessica.'

She knew there was some adult talk about to go on whenever Mum looked at her like that. They thought she didn't know the *big* secret, but she did. She knew Uncle Jack and Aunty Susan couldn't have babies. She'd heard Aunty Susan talking to Mum and it made Jessica very sad, so she liked to pretend that she was their little girl, a proper family, with Uncle Jack and Aunty Susan. They both spoilt her, and she knew Uncle Jack loved to play with her.

'Uncle Jack will take you to the beach this afternoon. Go and read that nice book I bought you last week, the one with the pussy cat on the front,' Mum said, widening her eyes and throwing them towards the stairs.

Jessica clambered to the half landing and flung herself into the spare bedroom, headlong onto the makeshift bed on the floor. She liked sleeping in the same room as her mum whenever they stayed at her aunt and uncle's house. She curled herself up into the tangled sheets that smelt of their home, Aunty Susan's perfume and Uncle Jack's tobacco.

Jessica loved playing on the beach, especially in the sand dunes. They were brilliant for hide and seek and the other games she played with Uncle Jack. He loved it too, she could tell, especially when he hugged her tight. Mum and Aunty Susan were also happy. They could go to bingo or do their shopping when Uncle Jack took Jessica out, taking her little hand into his big one, just like a real daddy would. Uncle Jack encouraged Mum and Aunty Susan to go shopping, giving them piles of money from his pockets full of pound notes and silver coins.

'Come and find a sweetie,' he'd tease Jessica once they'd gone, putting her hand into his trouser pocket. He told her she'd find a surprise tight in the folds, right in the corners, so she had to dig deep. He'd smile wide and wink at her as she found the sweeties.

She loved the black wavy hair that fell to his shoulders, just like the singer from Bay City Rollers. He even had the same blue eyes. Jessica wanted to marry a man just like Uncle Jack when she was grown up. She didn't mind that he smoked a lot, but she did try to hold his other hand, the one without the smelly yellow fingers.

Uncle Jack played exciting adventures, made up silly voices and pirate stories, and made Jessica the princess that he would have to find and rescue. Mum would laugh. Jessica knew Mum thought Uncle Jack was her perfect babysitter, and everyone was happy.

I WISH THEY'D come soon. I'm really, really cold.

Jessica's thoughts floated up into the new morning air. The fresh breeze of another day tempted and teased the long-tufted strands of grass, whipping up a melody, encouraging sea birds to circle and caw above her. The whispering sand grasses sang solemn music and played her a lovely lament.

The grey sea crashed onto the beach and sent a barrel-drum rolling towards her. It gave her a feeling of a tummy rumble and deep rattle inside her. She thought of the big white rolling waves. If only they would come, reach out to her, make her wet and free and carry her back to the flat beach, uncovered and in the open air. But they would never reach her. The old air-raid shelters, with their thick heavy bricks, now collapsed and scattered wide over the sand dunes were too far from the edge of the sea.

'Hello! Hello!' She tried to shout out. *'Hey!'*

But nobody came, and nobody heard, and nobody saw.

A LITTLE LATER, a group of older kids arrived. They lounged on top of the shelters and played rude games with each other. They neither heard nor saw little girl hidden beneath, under the half sunken slab of brick as they passed around their forbidden cigarettes and bottles of cider. When they'd finished their naughty games, they left, laughing and screeching. She felt abandoned again, like their dead cigarettes and empty bottles.

It was her fault Daddy went away. She sat listening on the stairs, waiting for Crossroads to finish and for Dr Who to start on their television. It was new and they'd never had a telly box before. She heard Uncle Jack talking to Mum and Aunty Susan.

'But she's so delightful.' His deep voice made her feel warm.

'She is, but he couldn't deal with her.'

'It's not her fault.' Uncle Jack stuck up for her. He always did.

'I know that, but he wanted a son, Jack, and when it happened...' Her mum's voice broke off, quiet and sad.

Aunty Susan snorted. 'He should have stuck with you, both of you, not left. What sort of man is that?' Aunty Susan liked to tell everyone what sort of man she thought Jessica's father was.

She didn't want to listen again how she survived, and her twin brother didn't.

'It was too much responsibility, Susan,' her mother said, like she always said.

Jessica ran upstairs, trying to be quiet and stop the tears that burnt her cheeks. Jessica knew she'd made Daddy go, that it was all her fault, she was too much responsibility, and it was because she was a girl and not a boy.

She wondered if that was why Uncle Jack was so kind to her. Sometimes, she wished he wouldn't try so hard. Jessica was no longer sure she liked some of his games, but she knew she couldn't say so, because he might go away, just like Daddy did.

JESSICA FOUND A friend, a transient companion. '*You wouldn't believe how much litter people leave on the beach.*'

The tired bird, in need of a rest, trilled. 'Coo.'

'Big winds blow things into here, my little home, so you be careful,' she warned the pretty racing pigeon.

The derelict air-raid shelter was crammed with empty cartons, battered cans, slick strands of seaweed, and assorted debris left on the beach, lost or discarded by day trippers oblivious to what lay around them.

'Uncle Jack cleared it out for us, making it nice for us to play, but it hasn't been tidied for such a long time. Sorry it's a bit smelly.'

'Coo, coo.'

'I know all about wildlife while I've been waiting. More than I did at school. Did you know there are sand mice?'

'Coo…Coo…' The lost bird hopped. It's bobbing his head pecked around Jessica.

'There are tons of insects and spiders. Some don't come near me and I'm so glad for that! Some tickle me when they walk up my legs or crawl behind my ears. They climb on me when they think I'm not looking.'

She remembered Uncle Jim tickling her. That's how he started. She laughed in the beginning, joining in, liking the game. She wouldn't laugh now, now that she knew better. And she wouldn't put her hands in his pockets either!

'There was this huge animal. I don't know what it was, you'd better look out for it...' she warned the bird who was ignoring her.

'...that thing that made a terrible nest in my hair! But it's gone now. Horrible! When the babies were born, they wriggled about lots and it felt like they were right inside my head.'

The bird squeezed out into sunshine and flew off, leaving Jessica to think on her own for another day.

'I'll teach her to swim.'

'Ooh, thanks, Jack! She'll love that.'

'Kelly will be so jealous!' Jessica squealed, eyes bright, thinking of her best friend and hugging Uncle Jack tight. Jessica loved the water.

My Uncle Jack, teaching me to swim! She couldn't wait to go back to the beach again.

'WOOF. WOOF.'

'Hello! What's your name?'

'Woof. Woof.'

A piece of her clothing flapped in sun, poking through one of the gaps between the rock and the sand. A large dog scrabbled over to her and put his wet nose on the light pink material. He tugged it all the way through the gap and away from her body. The dog howled and ran off.

'You could have stayed. Sniffed me some more,' Jessica called, but he was gone.

'*What time is it? Are you here yet?*' And nobody answered. Nobody every answered her. It was another sad day.

When at last they did come, Jessica tried to speak.

How old am I now? I'm in Mrs Robertson's class and my best friend is Kelly Brown. I was born on the third of October 1967. Jessica, that's my name. I was nearly seven when Uncle Jim left me here. How old am I now?

HER OPAQUE EYES looked at them, but she didn't see, and they didn't hear her.

He was teaching me to swim, my Uncle Jack. It was easy for him in the water, to do his things where no one could see. He pretended he was holding me up, making me steady. No one could see his hand, or his fingers. When I learnt to swim, I didn't need holding up anymore and I could do it on my own so he showed me other tricks, like surfing the waves. He liked to practice the movements on me first, when we were in our shelter. Then he took me to the sea and the practice was real. He would put it inside me, again and again, until the white froth came, and the sea would come and wash it all away.

Have you spoken to Uncle Jack? He probably would have cried and said he tried to save me from the water, from drowning, but couldn't because of the rough sea. I bet he said he lost me in the water. He did lose me in the water. He drowned me. Then he carried me to our little den where I lay cold, so very cold with my clothes almost gone. I have my pants on though. He put them back on me before he left. The rock he put on my tummy has kept them there, but it doesn't keep me warm. He put my pink T-shirt over my head but I'm glad it blew away. It was like a flag sending a signal because that big dog came took it. Is that how you found me? I'm glad you have found me. I don't want to be cold anymore. I don't like it on the beach.

Tiny Little Feet

I don't think they have a stated size for her. Her tiny heart pounds, less than the size of a grape, keeping her alive for another minute. She shouldn't be here yet, she's not ready. Blue veins, fragile but strong, pump blood through to her vital organs that struggle hard for her to survive.

A week ago, I could have had her legally terminated. Today, a delicate flower, attached to machines instead of to me, she lies in an incubator, breathing with the aid of pumped oxygen. Her little pink hat warms her head which smaller than a tennis ball. Her tiny eyes are shut tight. Her button mouth opens to a pin head gap as her body involuntary stretches. My eyes tingle with hot tears and love as I watch her sleep.

The nurse said I could touch her, but I dare not. I'm frightened she might break, disintegrate in my fingers like the dust she could have been last week, would have been last week had I not changed my mind. I'm so glad I did. Conceived in haste and displeasure, I did not want to hate her.

With an epiphany she was born anyway, so premature they didn't expect her to survive. It's a miracle she has. Hope surges through me, confidence that I can do this. My darling daughter has given this to me, with a fight and strength I never knew existed. I reach out and touch her through the gap in the hard plastic surround, my gloved hand shaking as I try to be more gentle than I've ever been before.

I count.

Two tiny little feet. Ten tiny little toes.

She's just perfect and she's all mine, and only mine. And I love her.

Golden Delicious

I'd been careless, I realise that now, but I couldn't help myself. She was so pretty with her curly golden hair that glistened when caught in the light. I wanted to reach out, to touch, to feel her soft skin and inhale her scent, so fresh and young.

With a month to go before her wedding, time was running out. I knew I had no chance, but I had to try. I imagined her wedding dress; beautiful, sequined, and virginal. Women only office staff were invited to her hen night out of town. A few lucky blokes may be hijacked on the night as part of the games they played on hen dos, but they'd be strangers, no threat. I told her I was away that weekend, invited or not. She didn't check, didn't care. I was nobody, just her boss.

THE DUSKY-PINK suede dress fell to the top of smooth knees, just a small gap between the hem and her skintight calf-length boots. I could almost taste her, sweet and sexy like a juicy peach. With the obligatory 'L' sticker adorning her back, like most 'hens' on their last night, it spoilt her image, sullied the occasion. My girl was better than that.

I loitered in the shadows, watching her laugh and topple as she became tipsy. I selected my vantage points and was hooded up in black, unseen, and sober, as I snapped pictures of her from a distance, my heart longing.

I needed a plan to get her away from the crowd. My palms were sticky, my head pulsating. I prayed for a chance as the church bell rang out midnight. The coach was picking them up at two o'clock. Time was running away.

An hour later I sat beneath a tree, a fair distance from the pub but I could see her, she was drunken flirting and resting her head on some guy's chest. I clenched and unclenched my fists and bit inside of my lower lip so much that I could taste blood.

Some of the crowd left the pub and wandered off down the street. Another girl followed, chasing after them, holding her shoes as she ran. That left three of the original group. I watched as she kissed the guy she'd been flirting with, right on his lips. My stomach flipped upside down.

It meant nothing.

She was only saying goodbye.

Good girl. Here she came.

My heartbeat was pounding, a strong rhythm beating in my ears. I glanced down the street and saw her friends filtering away. I moved across the road and hid behind the fence of a large house. She staggered out of the pub door, just a hundred yards away, and I leapt back out of sight. It was time.

As she passed by, I whispered loud enough to attract her attention, 'Kelly!'

She stopped.

I moved out of the dark, staying level with the fence. I didn't want to risk being seen by anyone else.

'Hi Kelly! It's me.'

She turned, swaying towards me. 'Hi!' Her eyes raised, as if trying to focus in the dark.

'Having a good time?' I asked, calm, chilled, hands splayed by my sides.

'Yes.' She wobbled. 'I thought you were away this weekend?'

'I changed my mind.'

Swaying, she said, 'Have you seen the others?'

'No,' I had to lie. 'You look fantastic. Here, let me take your photo.'

'But I need to find them.'

'One for the album, go on,' I smooth talked her. 'I'll help you find the others, just let me take your picture. You're a natural, Kelly.'

She blushed. 'Oh, go on then.'

She smiled, all white teeth and unruly hair, a true picture of beauty. I took a few snaps and reached out to hold her steady as she wobbled. My eyes closed slowly as I felt her soft skin. A waft of perfume mingled with warm woman hit me.

'I don't want to miss the bus,' she slurred.

The cool night was helping the alcohol take effect.

'Doesn't matter, I can give you a lift.' I was her saviour.

She looked up and smiled as she leant backwards, eyes half closed. 'That's nice.'

Easy. I turned her round and we walked away from the main street where the rest of the crowd had gone. The booze was disorienting her, an added advantage, just as I hoped. I led her to my car, earlier parked in a strategic position, out of the way of any CCTV.

'I'll take you right to the doorstep,' I told her.

She climbed in and I took her little bag and leant across the seat to strap her in. Being so close to her made me light-headed, tingled me. I walked round to the driver's side, the cool night air calming my impatience. I retrieved her mobile from the pink silky purse and turned it off. I slid it into my pocket.

Her eyes closed and I could have kissed her. We were soon on the road out of town. I imagined running my fingers through her loose hair as she lolled against the headrest.

She interrupted my fantasy when she sat up. 'I'm hungry. Can we stop? Pick up something to eat?'

It was the last thing I wanted. 'I'm staying not far from here. We can call into my place and get something there.'

'Great, thanks. I should try to call the others, let them know where I am.' She bent down for her purse by her feet. She scrabbled in the foot well.

'My phone! It was in my bag. It's gone. I must have lost it. Damn!'

Easy. With sympathetic noises, I apologised for not having my own phone with me. A few minutes later, I turned into the lane.

'It's very dark. I'm cold,' she said, shivering. 'You live up here?'

'No, it's where I'm staying. I like to take off and do a bit of photography.'

She accepted the excuse.

A tremor of excitement shot through me as I pulled up and killed the engine. A copse of trees hid my two-man tent. Animals coo-ed and softly grunted in the background. An owl hooted as the engine ticked.

'We won't be long, will we? Just that Phil's expecting me back soon and the others will wonder where I am.' She shivered some more.

'Just over here,' I pointed.

I opened the car door, stepped out, and made my way to the passenger side. I opened her door and reached out to take her hand. I pulled her up and she rose and put a leg out of the car. She fell into me and held her with a determined grip as she stood, all the while resting into me.

'Oh! A tent!' Her face crumpled as she spoke. 'I thought it would be a cottage. Or something.'

'I like to get down and dirty.' I smiled at her. This was going to be fun.

We walked the few yards to the tent. I unzipped the front, reached in, and pulled out a blanket that I handed to her. 'There's not much in the way of food. I've got some malt loaf, a banana, an apple…'

'Just the apple thanks.' She took it with a shrug. 'Can we go now, Sandra? Please?'

THAT'S WAS HOW easy it was. When I'd finished, I packed up, disguised my tracks, left no trace.

Except for the apple. She'd only taken a bite, one bite, and so had I, before throwing it into the nearby trees. I'd been so careful. The only way they traced me was my DNA from the apple and my unique malocclusion bite. I'd have got away with it if wasn't for the damn apple.

Every time, it's the goddamn apple. Just ask Adam.

A Man Called Andy

He ordered a blender online and acted like it was the best thing to happen in his life. Okay, he had done it all himself, placed the bid in the last few seconds, and it was his, on his own and without my help. It seemed to be the most hotly anticipated device of the year, nay the century. It was only a food mixer for Christ's sake, and it would impact on the surface of the kitchen, using up more of the little space we had in the tiniest room in the flat.

But Andy didn't care.

I knew we had something similar buried in the basement, in the corner that Beth, who owned the building and lived downstairs, had allocated to us, but I didn't want to go rooting through cobwebs, spiders, *Dandy Annuals,* and shoes from the 80s' that would have shrunk in the storage. Andy had seemed so excited to find the Magimix, the type his mother had when he was a boy, that I didn't have it in me to tell him to look to see if the one in the cellar was any good.

I was worried about him but was I worried about him enough to care anymore? I did what I usually did in similar circumstances. I sighed.

'Andy, do we really need a blender?' I asked him three days later when it still hadn't arrived. I wish I hadn't bothered.

He told me of his grandiose plans of inviting the neighbours round for dinner, impressing anyone who would care to listen, strangers in the street, birds tweeting on the window ledge. We didn't speak to the neighbours. They barely knew of his existence and I doubted if they even knew our names. We were just that couple who lived here, kept ourselves to ourselves, a bit quiet, a bit insignificant. Some may say, a bit odd.

I knew I would have to do something soon and I knew it would be difficult. I didn't want to face it. I wanted to bury my head as far as I could in the dry deserts of Siberia. Or a bottle of cheap plonk. Anything but accept what I knew I would have to do. And soon.

THEY SAID HE would be fine, he would be okay in time, but time had passed, tick-tock, in slow motion, and he hadn't become fine. He'd become better, but he was far from fine. Then he deteriorated and I felt I had let him down. I knew it wasn't my fault, but I'd done nothing to help him and I'd done everything I could think of to help him. Whatever I did made no difference because there was nothing I could do to change things. I had a life, once. Today it was a struggle to hold down a job and to live the life we'd fallen into. When he'd bagged the eBay bargain, I did the cowardly thing and sighed and said it was fine. That word again. Fine. There was nothing fine about our life at all. It was a misrepresentation of a life I'd always wanted.

We'd always gone walking, in the park, up in the hills, down by the river. We'd even take the train to the mountains and go off hiking for the day. He used to love the fresh air that stung his face, filled his lungs with something other than city fug. He relished freedom, once. Before today.

The longer I left it, the longer I let it go on, the worse Andy got. I couldn't put it off any longer. I would have to make an appointment with his consultant and soon. But

I wasn't his wife – I was just a girl he'd made fall in love with him. Then he'd had the accident.

I did what I thought was the right thing and moved in with him. It took everything I had, but I loved the man with the floppy dark hair, the gorgeous welsh accent that made me melt inside and out, and the fingertips that set me on fire, and now that person no longer existed.

The only thing the doctors said was 'It'll take time.'

He wasn't Andy anymore. He was not the man I'd fallen in love with. He wasn't my responsibility and I hadn't taken any vows of in sickness and in health. Did that make me an awful person? I'd known him for such a short time. How could I be expected to look after him?

It was to be the holiday of our lifetime. He'd booked us an all-inclusive trip to Zell-am-Zee in Austria. I had a warm deep-down feeling inside that made me feel fuzzy and loved and like he was the man I was destined to spend the rest of my life with. He'd told my best friend that he had vowed never to marry but if anyone would make him change his mind, it would be me. She told me she thought he was going to propose. I believed her.

It would be the perfect setting, ski-ing down some of the best slopes in Europe and sipping a delicious gluewein afterwards by a flickering log fire. I had my answer prepared. I hadn't reckoned on an accident.

It was our second day. The snow was vast, sparkling like a thousand million diamonds in the winter sun. I guess the sun made the top layer a bit soft, a bit unreliable. It was our first run of the day. Would have been. The first run of the day.

We set off, smiled at each other, determined to make it a race to the bottom of the slope. We'd both skied before but my experience was limited to a school trip when I was fifteen. I'd begged my parents to let me go on when we really couldn't afford it. Andy, being the sporty type, was all but an expert. He'd had family holidays at Cloisters and had taken a gap year which included a three-month stay in the Italian Alps where he practised his slalom skills along with his bachelor techniques.

The guy came from nowhere. I don't know if he was a rogue skier, a deserter from a novice class, or a maverick, but he shot down behind us like a bullet. Dressed all in black and determined, he took Andy's legs from under him. Andy fell backwards and I laughed. At first. As his crooked body lay there and didn't move, I knew then it might be serious, something not to be laughed at. An instructor from a nearby class was with us in an instant. He knew what to do. I don't remember all of it now, a blur I'd rather forget. To think of it makes my head hurt and go to a different place I don't want visit for fear I won't come back.

When Andy fell, he banged his head. A bleed on the brain the doctors said. He was lucky to survive. Emergency surgery and pressure in his head and all sorts of other complications, but he lived. Unlike that poor actress a few weeks before him. Natasha Richardson. I admired her. I grieved for her. Then it happened to my Andy and I was bereft.

After his accident, Andy couldn't do his job anymore, so he lost it. He couldn't pay his bills anymore, so he lost his house. I found us a flat and tried hard to make it work. Then we had to move to this studio, at the top of a three-storey house with tiny crevices I converted into storage space with trips to Ikea to make our home practical. All the while Andy refused to go out, became more paranoid, spent more of my money on bargains we didn't need, filled the flat with useless eBay purchases.

His speech was stilted, his words muddled, and I felt more like his mother than a lover. I'd stopped being his lover a long time ago when he said he couldn't do the sex thing anymore. It was like he'd become a little boy again, but without the cuteness of an eight-year-old.

It was time. My day was done. I felt so selfish. For a non-Catholic, it was a good line in guilt, but I wasn't a martyr. There were many nights I felt like taking him by the hand and leading him through the streets of London and leaving him in a cardboard box with blankets and a stray dog. I imagined tucking him in tight and kissing him goodnight-goodbye, but I could never do that. I wasn't cruel.

I resolve to do what I have to do. The residential home said they would take him when the time was right. It was time for him to go. I will do it. I will make the call.

Tomorrow.

Slicing Onions

My earliest memory of Mum slicing onions was one lunchtime when I came home from school and she was sitting on our threadbare settee, crying. When I asked her what was wrong, she folded a letter into her pinny pocket and sniffed, 'Nothing love, just slicing onions.'

I had tomato soup and bread ducks for lunch and knew it didn't have any onions in it, but by the time I went back to school for the afternoon, I'd forgotten about onions and couldn't wait for an afternoon of painting and playing skips with my best friend, Dotty.

Mum sliced onions a lot around the time Dad stopped coming home.

TEN YEARS LATER, I returned home from school after taking an exam to find Mum crying. She said she was slicing onions. I pointed out that ham sandwiches and carrot cake didn't have onions. She patted my arm like I should know better.

Three days later, Nan died and although I never saw Mum slice any onions, she cried a lot.

When I told Mum that I'd passed all my A levels and had a place at university, I saw the tears fall from her glistening eyes. 'Only slicing onions love,' she said, smiling at me.

She sliced onions on my wedding day and again a few years later when I gave birth to twin girls.

THIRTY YEARS AFTER I first found Mum slicing onions, my daughters ask me, 'Why are you crying Mummy?'

They are four years old. I sniff and remember a day, so many years ago, when I had tomato soup from a tin and little bread ducks, and I learnt about slicing onions for the first time.

I think of Mum and how I'll never see her again but how proud of me she was.

I smile at my concerned daughters' faces and tell them,

'Only slicing onions girls,' and I hug them tight.

A Way with the Kids

Silence hovered, hesitant, waiting to be cracked open. Like a baby's first breath, as an offering, the infant cried. A boy or a girl, I know now that it was neither and I didn't care. I couldn't. I was the messenger.

The church clock chimed a notification to those who would remember today, and plenty of the village would. The ringing of the hour was ignored by those asleep or oblivious to calling of the church. Eight strikes rang, alerting those who knew the bell tower, like religion, was out of kilter. It was six o'clock. After today, the clock would be righted to fix the changes and smooth the calm in the small fractured community.

After laying the tightly wrapped muslin package on the doorstep of the church, I moved away, past the stone wall and waited. Nobody came for collection in the churchyard on this crisp Christmas morning for it was too cold for even the ants to dance at dawn.

At the true hour of eight, the crying was no longer. Dawn break sun had disappeared, and dark clouds gathered. My cold skin shivered and body shuddered as I felt something lift and leave this village. The baby would cry no more. Unmoving, I waited.

A feather whipped along, carried by a light wind. It settled on the wrapped-up babe. White, jaunty, and brazen, it gave the closed tight face a tickle as it paused. Nothing; no reaction, no sign of movement, no little breaths to push it away and stillness reigned. Then the breeze lifted, bobbing the feather along once more.

Reverend Peyote entered the stone-cold church around nine o'clock via the vestry entrance. Heating pipes were to be warmed, bread to be placed, wine to be aired. I watched the church come alive as he lit candles. When he came outside carrying a bag of rubbish to the large black bin, I heard him hum a Christmas Carol. 'Away in a Manger'. It was a favourite from childhood, many eons ago. I smiled and wondered at the innocence and ignorance of my past.

Half an hour later, the Reverend was joined by his chosen church wardens, his own personal flock. They also entered via the vestry, making my wait longer. When the clock struck twelve, the people at home prepared themselves for the ten thirty service. The congregation would be heavy today and I knew my wait would soon be over. As the wind grew and the black clouds congregated, so did the people making their way to church.

Still the body lay.

'Hold on to your hats, ladies,' called Mr Thomas the local butcher, as his once a year fedora flew from his head. Running after it with a skip, his tick-tack heels hurried him along the gravel drive ahead of the crowd. His hat settled atop the bundle on the step at the front of the church.

'Bejesus!' He cursed. He held out his hand to halt the gossiping women making their way towards him. He shouted, 'Stop! Go and fetch Reverend Peyote. Please.'

Job done, I slipped away.

INFILTRATION HAD BEEN easy. Debra Makin; eager, willing, and simple, she came cheap. Befriending a lonesome mother who had been done and dumped was a gas. Two days of chit, chat, and sympathy, she was ready when she drank the sweet tea I gave her. I wiped the last forty-eight hours from her memory as she fell into slumber. I let my lips brush her cheek and apologised for what had to be done.

The serrated seven-inch knife with her prints on the handle lay discarded on the cluttered coffee table. The deep stab wounds found in the baby, the slashes on her own thin body, the bizarre ink drawings discovered in her notebooks; they all pointed to her. She'd lost it.

Debra Makin wouldn't remember being unable to cope with severe post-natal depression, or that she believed her boy to be the Devil Child. She wouldn't recall slicing and stabbing his abdomen, running the blade under his chin, down his body, and cutting off his genitals. She would forget that she'd daubed his rich red blood on the walls of her sparse apartment, the words 'Devil Child' emblazoned for all to see. She would forget about taking her baby to the steps of the church for redemption.

When they told her she was the one responsible, she wouldn't believe it. Would deny all knowledge. She would protest her innocence and would tell them she would have loved her son and never harm him, ever. She would be unable to convince the authorities and be pilloried in the community and forever be unwelcome, having committed the ultimate sin. The courts would order that she be placed in a psychiatric unit to repent her unforgivable sins.

Without any other explanation, she'd begin to accept the horror of what she must have done and be unable to forgive herself. They would find her, covered in strange smelling faeces and strangled in her cell, sheets wrapped around her neck in a bizarre suicide; another sign of her guilt and evidence of her madness.

In reality, she'd become just another lost soul in the world we had to redeem.

ELIMINATION OF INFILTRATED EXISTENCES (EIE), an essential but unknown and secretive agency belonging to all the world governments lay hidden in the annals of every defence department.

The Cleansing Section cleared my tracks and eradicated the sinful house of my presence. They also made sure the world would continue to condemn the psychotic mother, keeping the story alive in the world's media.

The Department researchers were about to allocate me my next assignment while my colleagues in the special task force of Eliminators, like me, conducted their own secretive missions, obliterating sociopathic, psychopathic, and other such 'paths from the infiltrated world.

With my latest task complete, I moved on to Albany, New York, to await full details of my next assignment, #303. I didn't like to do the innocents, had done enough young ones in the years I'd given, but my boss said, 'We reserve these cases for you. You've got a way with the kids.'

I wasn't sure what he meant, whether to be flattered or floored.

'There's a little girl with blonde bobbing curls and a sweet smile. She's shown the signs.' He sent me the file.

I rattled the shards of ice in my tumbler, swirling the honey coloured liquor first right, then left as I looked through the dossier. The chilled bittersweet taste of liquor burnt my throat as I read.

Last month this little girl had been responsible for killing her neighbour's hamster by squeezing it to death for fun. She'd put rat poison into the fish tank when visiting her grandfather. A week ago, she'd broken her baby brother's arm by twisting it as he lay in his crib, asleep. Her parents awoke to guffaws of screeching laughter that drowned out their son's painful screams.

My boss thinks that a sudden impact death would be best. Perhaps a deviation into the path of truck when she's on her new pink tricycle, the one she was given for her fourth birthday. She'd wanted a black trike, but her parents had bought her pink, trying to make her more like a pretty princess than a dark prince. They were aware of course, like most kin, of the evil lurking within but sweet candy colours would do nothing for her, despite their best efforts.

The Department found out that Maria would be a future female serial-killer, one with a penchant for pretty young boys with a malicious taste for torturing them. The holographic photos of the future dismembered bodies, those potential victims not yet born, they keep me awake long into the night.

While I figure out what I'm going to do with her, I think back to that baby.

It isn't nice when good turns bad. They could have been such a lovely little family. The woman, she'd been quite attractive in a cheap sort of way, with her dazzling blue eyes and coffee coloured skin coated in butterscotch moisturiser. In a different world, I might have liked her. Sacrificing a mother, a young girl who knew no better, it had to be done. She might have borne another babe in the future, one like that which she'd already given life to, so she had to be eradicated. Such a shame, but Saddam couldn't be allowed to survive again. He had to be eliminated. In his case, infanticide was for the best.

Killing kiddies is such a dreadful way to make a living. It's such an ugly thing to do but someone has to do it when you have the world to save.

You Can't Change Time

In my twenties I thought death was so far away it needn't concern me. Death was for old people, ill people, those about-to-die people. It wasn't for me.

I'd had plenty of grief from various sources to satisfy my depressive, maudlin, pessimism but personal experience of close death was to elude me for a long time. Over the years, I'd stand at the back of a church or crematorium, stand at the side of a non-religious graveside, be present at the committal of various acquaintances and even some relative strangers. I'd weep for the loss that belonged to those left behind. The wind would dry my tears and I'd pull on my gloves as I left the mourners to their grief, grateful that it wasn't mine. I felt like I'd stolen their sorrow, intruded and cried when I had no right to do so and I felt their loss like it could have been my own. I was thankful it never was.

ALL OF A SUDDEN, my husband and I looked back and smiled. We hadn't done a bad job. We had become happy, watched our children have their children and live different lives. We grew into grandparents of the sort I imagined children should have. Our life had come right after years of struggles. This was our time.

Then came the cancer and death was no longer a stranger.

HE LOVED THE winter when rich reds, burnt oranges, and burnished browns filled the skies as the leaves turned and fell, leaving the barren bones of trees. We booked our beautiful mountainside cottage with views over the tumbling river where white-water rafting took place all year round and mysterious mists wrapped around majestic mountains and hung in mid-air.

Tall rich-green pines lined the motorway before the country lane turn off. Wood-smoke filled the crisp air that filtered through the vents as we travelled towards our final destination.

He turned to me, smiling, eyes bright and said, 'Thank you.'

'What for, you silly beggar?' I laughed, twisting the steering wheel to the left and quickly right to avoid the stag that stood brave in our path. I manoeuvred my way past him and drove on, a lonesome car on a deserted wintery lane.

My husband placed a hand on mine as I manipulated the gears of our new car and he squeezed my fingers. 'For bringing me here. Just the two of us…for one last time.'

Then he looked away from me and I watched him soak up the surrounding beauty, trying not to miss a thing. I swallowed hard, unable to speak, not knowing what to say.

As if reading my mind, he said, 'It's okay. It's time…and you can't change time.'

I knew he'd accepted it even though I was still trying to fight. I willed the hot tears to stay as I drove with watery eyes for the rest of the journey.

The owners of the cottage had lit a fire, for which I was thankful. They said they didn't mind us coming to stay two days, two weeks, or however long we wanted. However long it took. It was their privilege, they said. It was a quiet time, winter, and we could have their cottage for as long as we needed.

One bedroom, one kitchen, one bathroom, one living room. The living room. The room people lived in. A living room. One fireplace, one settee, one table with one vase and a bunch of winter-white flowers. And one bed. A bed. Pushed against the wall beside the fire, underneath the window with the best view, the one that looked out towards the river, the mountains, the mists, and the moonlight. It was no longer a living room. It would become a dying room.

I made tea, spooning sugar into my cup, a new thing since I'd started to think about death. A sweetener, of sorts. It wasn't supposed to be this way. Not now, not when we'd got properly happy. I sipped my tea and let his go cold. I knew he couldn't drink it but still I made two cups, like always. A habit. I wondered how long I'd go on making two cups of tea.

'Thank you,' he whispered as I helped him lay back so he could sink down into the bed with the warmed sheets that were lit by a low lamp to his side. 'Thank you, for the best years of my life.'

I said, 'No, I thank you,' and kissed his lips as he fell asleep. The journey had exhausted him and soon, far too soon, it would be over, his journey complete.

I watched dusk settle and listened to the crackle of the fire. It needed another log, but I didn't want to move from my where I sat, looking out of the window and holding his hand as he slept. Then darkness fell and, on that day, there was no news.

THE NEXT DAY we talked, when he could, and we remembered. And the day after that. On the third day we talked some more, when he stirred and woke for short bursts of time. He asked me to tell him about how we met. By accident. A quirk of fate. I reminded him that he had delivered boxes to my office by mistake. He'd taken my telephone number just in case he got lost again. He smiled then, when I told him that. And of course, he rang, like I knew he would. He told me he needed to find his way. Would I help him? Corny, but I told him we'd find it together.

I told him about our wedding, the birth of our children, the holidays in the caravan in Cornwall when the roof fell in and we were flooded. I told him about our children's lives and how we managed without help from either of our extended families because we had to. About the children leaving home and how we learnt to rely upon each other again, to love and hate each other at the same time like you do when you're going to survive any sort of marriage. We looked at the photographs we had brought with us so we could share the times again, for one last time, remembering together. And then he asked me – the thing I hoped he never would.

'Did you ever…with him?'

I knew what he was asking. I looked at him, at the love in his eyes and I didn't say anything.

He turned his head to the side. 'I found your note.'

I'd never sent it but put it in the back of a notebook. I remembered every word.

Do me a favour. Please don't come to my house anymore.

I look at you and you look back and your eyes make my stomach flip. I lurch towards you and feel your pull. You grin and my heart lifts.

A flight of fancy. Don't be silly, I tell myself. I try to dismiss you in my mind long after you have gone.

You came back today, smartly dressed, out of the rough work clothes. I didn't immediately recognise you with a shirt and tie until I looked up into your eyes. The shade of blue with the radiating grey welcoming me. I know you felt it too, that spark between us.

You came into my house to measure up for the jobs to be done. I saw your rippling muscles through your white shirt as you worked. I wanted to reach out and touch.

Please don't come again. I won't be able to help myself. I'm a married woman.

I TOLD MY husband the only thing I could. 'You are the only man I have ever loved.'

He smiled and squeezed my hand. He said he wanted to sleep, that it was time to go now. I talked to him, soothed him and made him comfortable all that day and long into the night when the fire had died, and the wood had turned to ash. I stroked his hair and held his body when he took his last breath.

And then Death became a reality and it hurt, so painful and so bad and it was here and now and not so far away after all and I was no longer twenty, but sixty and approaching the winter of my life, just like my husband had reached his. And then I knew for real, that you can't change time.

I was still sitting there when the dawn broke and I looked out to the tumbling river, to the majestic mountains with the mists hanging mysteriously in mid-air. And I saw him. The stag. Standing proud in the field, looking back at me. And I knew.

He would be with me forever.

Face in the Window

With eyes as bright as saucers he looked straight at the moon through the open skylight. His frozen fingers couldn't quite reach the clasp to close the frost-etched window.

He didn't know how many hours or days it had been, and it mattered not for he couldn't yet count. A bare but stained single mattress lay on the woodworm-ridden floorboards. He moved across the floor and tried to crawl under it, just as he had tried yesterday, and again he failed. He was so little, too frail, it wasn't possible.

He looked around the room, at the scratched walls where he had picked at the paper. The diamond-patterned wallpaper was the only thing he'd eaten since he had been put in the room and now it was gone. There was nothing left.

The acrid stench of urine didn't bother him anymore for he had become used to the smell of the room hidden in the eaves, the bare room with no toilet, only a corner he couldn't flush.

During the day weak sun played with him, teasing him with sun drops that didn't quite warm. At night stars twinkled with broken promises.

This freezing evening, he crawled into the darkest corner. The heat from the next house in the terrace gently seeped through tiny cracks. His knees rested tight against his chest, up against his naked body, and held by arms he could barely sense existed. He urinated. The smell was strong, but the warmth comforted him. Tiredness took over as his eyelids fell and his eyes closed.

Tomorrow. He hoped somebody would come tomorrow.

A Kind of Loving

I picked him up on a park bench and offered him a tissue with a sympathetic smile. He took both.

That was the beginning of our relationship and I held the power in my curled-up fist. Understanding and compassion made him come to me, he couldn't resist. My craft had been practised over many years and I was good at spotting the vulnerable ones.

We met in secret for weeks until he eventually built up the confidence and took me home. It was his choice. It always had to be their choice, with them leading the pace. I liked the ones from the well-off families best. They ignored their kids and gave them money and presents and pets to keep them amused, anything other than their personal time. It was no wonder these children were receptive to me.

THIS ONE, DANNY Young, he unfortunately came from the scummy kind, the sort of family that didn't care where their kids were so long as they weren't hanging around the house. This sort of family didn't have the cash to flash. It all went on fags, cheap beer, and the odd bit of whizz. The posh ones called it neglect, but they were equally bad. They might have had fancy cars and big houses, but they never gave the attention that the children craved or deserved.

This left the door nicely open for me.

DANNY'S MOTHER WAS living with his father's brother. His dad lived round the corner and came round every day. Two of his oldest brothers were inside for all manner of delinquency and his two youngest ones were heading that way. His sister was pregnant at fourteen and now at twenty, had three kids. All had the same dad which was a rarity in their family, but he'd not long left. They lived in the next street. Danny often stayed with her until she found a smack-head boyfriend who beat the crap out of him. That's when I found Danny, sitting on that bench, and I stepped in.

A kind of grooming, the officials call it. For me, it's a kind of loving.

None of them cared about him but they liked me, didn't doubt me. I told them I'd been a youth worker in the town I'd previously lived in and they had no reason to disbelieve it. It was a sort of truth, anyway. They liked my influence on Danny. He now had some manners and I taught him that it was best to help out at home and no one would be on his back if he behaved himself. It worked and they didn't bother about me taking him out here and there. They liked it, especially when I hired a minibus and took them all out for the day. It nearly killed me to do it, but it was worth it. I became a trusted friend and took Danny places his family couldn't, bought him things his family wouldn't. He was out of their way and they liked me, trusted me, and even encouraged me.

I'd slip him a fiver now and again and Danny was grateful. I bought him a new pair of trainers, the kind he'd never had. When he had a school photo taken and wanted to ditch it because no one would want it anyway, I bought the full pack and put one on my car dashboard. He saw it on my computer desktop too, when he came to visit for the first time. He blushed and thanked me.

It was easy after that. He was all mine.

I SUPPOSE I became greedy, complacent. One night it was getting very late and we'd been looking at porn on the computer. Between us, we'd drunk a bottle of wine, more him than me, but I couldn't drive having had more than one drink. He wanted to stay the night, so I let him. It was simple.

IT WAS A step too far.

The next day, as I pulled into the petrol station for refuelling, a police car pulled up alongside us. It didn't bother me, but Danny looked uneasy. I gave him the money and sent him in to pay. The female cop followed but only to buy a paper. Danny panicked and made a run for it through the emergency exit, out the back door, and straight into a courtyard.

Of course, they were suspicious. He looked guilty and acted guilty. They checked him out, then me. I could tell she knew, that female cop. I saw her look at Danny's photo on my dash. She questioned me, eyes narrowed, distrustful. She asked if I loved him. Cheek! Of course, I did, but I wasn't going to give it away, that would be telling.

Now, sitting my cell, I have to admit, that Danny was different. He was gentle and kind. Not rough like his undeserving family. I could have given him such a better life. If only it was after his sixteenth birthday, they wouldn't have bothered checking me.

I very nearly had him for good. One step at a time and gently does it. He'd have been mine forever. His family would have willingly given him up to live with me, come his birthday. It was one less kid for them to worry about.

The first time they caught me I'd been teaching young boys to swim. I took them to the top and then they'd jump in from the highest rung. They look so goddamn handsome in their little swimming trunks; I couldn't help myself.

I learnt to pick older targets after that and there were so many. After all, adolescent boys are so grateful for any outlet for their raging hormones.

And nobody suspected a middle-aged female until they did.

A Gypsy Woman Told My Mother

Awizened old gypsy woman told my mother that my son would be forever young. I laughed. They were as bad as each other; mother for going to the damn woman in the first place and the crabbity old woman for feeding gullible grandmas bowls of tripe.

'Oh, but she was serious, Jane!' my mother said across the long-distance line from Turkey.

'I'm sure she was but I don't think you should go and see her again,' I told her.

Mother tutted and I imagined her folding her arms and twisting her lips in a grimace. I knew she'd be thinking it should be the other way around, her telling me what not to do. I also imagined her asking herself, who is the mother here? I'd heard it all before. Ever since she'd retired to the far-off lands in search of a secret toy boy, I knew the roles would reverse. I also knew she'd go back to the old woman up in the hills beyond Aydin.

A week later my mother rang again. The gypsy woman had told her more. She knew my littlest girl, Alice, bit her nails. Mother didn't know this fact. She had last seen Alice as a baby and now my little girl was four. The old woman knew my eldest daughter, Isobel, had dark hair when she was born but it had long since turned blond. She said her hair would turn back to black. By bottle or age, she didn't say. This girl, the brightest star, would do wondrous things and be very successful. I tutted.

Then mother threw the curve ball. My own fate was damning. The soothsayer told my mother I had a lot of stress to come at work and it would last for four years, after which I would smile again. I foolishly laughed when my mother relayed this to me. I always had stress at work.

'Oh, no dear, she meant something more than that. Something sinister is afoot. Be wary of big men in suits.'

I laughed some more. They were all big suits where I worked.

I heard hesitation crack in her voice when she asked, 'How's Michael?'

'Fine.' I didn't want to pursue this any longer. A shiver prickled down my back. In between our last conversation and this, Michael had a dream. Hearing my little boy cry out in the early hours was unusual. Since their dad died, I'd looked after our three children as best as I could. I couldn't help being protective and I rushed to his bedside in a panic. He clung to me, his young fingers turning white at the knuckle. I smelt his fear like a wild animal caught with nowhere to go. He'd dreamt that when he was a big boy, eighteen or something he said, and a lorry would run him over. Then he sobbed. 'You'll always be in my heart, Mummy.'

He clenched his little hand and banged his fist on his chest. 'Always in here, Mummy.'

I tried to change the subject. 'What are you doing tonight, Mum?'

'The old woman told that me he'd always be in your heart,' she replied.

My stomach flipped and the cold trickle ran through my heart. 'She's filling your head with rubbish.' I couldn't help but be angry with her. This wasn't a road I wanted to travel. 'Please mother, don't go to see her again…or if you do, please don't tell me about it.'

I WASN'T ONE for hocus-pocus soothsaying, but I have to be honest and confess to a feeling of unease that lasted a number of years. From time to time my mind would flick to my mother and her gypsy woman.

Her prophecy of stress at work came true. The big suits ousted me when I challenged them on the finances of the company. I learnt it doesn't pay to tell the boss he might have it wrong. They paid me off, the best option for us both. It was a difficult few years, but it turned out to be the best thing to ever have happened. When I realised this, Ireland beckoned me, inviting me to start of a new life with my growing-up family.

I never heard any more about the old gypsy women in the hills past Aydin. Mother died and we mourned her greatly. The children turned into teens and for a while our family home turned into a battle-worn castle but as these things do, they settled down.

Isobel went off to Dublin to study medicine, complete with long black goth hair and a great and bright future ahead of her. My mother would have been proud. Her father certainly would have been. Isobel and I cried sad sweet tears the day she left.

Alice grew out of biting her nails and grew them long and strong. She was turning into a wilful teen, but she kept me balanced with her good humour and ready smile. She delivered a quick line in retort, just like her father, and I was secretly pleased to see it.

Michael, our son, was strapping and big-hearted and due to go off to Aberdeen University to study English and History. He fancied becoming a historian but thought it might be a bit out-dated. The advent of historical documentaries, historical dramas and going back-to-the-past genealogy had made it fashionable to study history once more, so he decided not to worry about it too much for now. He said that if he doesn't make it, he could teach. He loves kids. Ever the optimist and not unlike his father, he wouldn't see it as failing.

THE DAY WAS hot and long. We had deposit some of Michael's possessions at the halls of residence. On the way home, we stopped off at Dunattor Castle. Michael was interested in the history of the ruins which were said to date as far back as 5AD, maybe earlier. He was keen to learn more about the mysterious green lady ghost.

'You're just like your nan, Michael…though she would have come for the ghost and the brew, not at all interested in the history.' I linked arm in arm with my handsome son. His floppy blond hair hung across his eyes and he crinkled his eyes and his smile at me.

'It's all right, Mum, I won't let the green lady haunt you.' He laughed.

So, did I, at my disbelief of all things ghostly.

He flicked through the pamphlet, pausing to read, 'The spirit of the green lady has been seen in the brewery at the Castle. She is said to be looking for her "lost children" who are the Picts who converted from her religion to Christianity around the 5th Century AD.'

I looked at him, saw his mind at work and loved the way he was so enrapt. I could see the passion light his eyes and I knew with certainty that he would do well. We spent a delightful couple of hours and as dark clouds scudded the sky, it was time for us to leave.

IT TOOK A couple of hours to reach our turn off from the main road and darkness was complete. I'd wanted to be back at our rented cottage earlier. I hated driving along country lanes in the black of night. The last twelve miles were up and down, twisting and turning, and I struggled to avoid roadkill. Not my idea of fun. At least it wasn't raining. If only Michael had his licence, he could have driven.

I changed gears to negotiate the coming bend, the comfortable silence between us reassuring. It wouldn't be long before Michael would be self-sufficient though I bet he'd still be bringing his washing home for Mum. I might be lonely with one child left at home, but it would be great to watch them forge their own lives.

The waft of mist as I took the bend surprised me. It had been such a bright day and a clear night with sparkling stars. Like a fleeting ghost, evaporating quicker than water on the pavement on a hot day, it was gone. I looked at the milometer and saw we had another eight miles for home.

'What did you make of that?' I said.

Michael didn't answer and I glanced across at him. His head was lolling against the window as he slumbered. He looked just like he had when he was a little boy. I had the urge to push his fringe back out of his sleeping eyes, but I had to turn to concentrate on the winding road ahead.

I drove up the hill, slowing down, aware of the turn into single track on the descent. As I negotiated the left-hand bend, the mist surrounded us once more. White, bright light, it felt like the car was floating off the ground. I couldn't see the road. I turned to look out of the side window, but the white cloud enclosed us. I looked down, out of the front window. I saw a street below and kids were playing on skateboards in daylight. There was Michael. Six-year-old Michael. It was the day he had fallen and grated his knee. It was bleeding and his dad was there, mopping up the flow of blood and smiling at his son. But that wasn't right. His dad had died a few years before that. He wasn't there when Michael had to have the stitches in his knee. Was he?

I gripped the steering wheel and pulled myself further towards the windscreen to try to get closer and see more. The scene in front of me changed. The cloud became denser, losing the fluffy marshmallow ridges.

Crisp caramel leaves surround me and I'm falling with autumn sycamore seeds caught in a spindrift, spinning, spinning fast. I reach out a hand, mine but not mine, fat fingers gyrating as the colours spin far away, falling too fast. A sparkling bright light blinds me with beauty. It means beauty. Serene Koh-I-Noor diamonds twinkle glass-sharp beauty, full of hope and dreams, twisting with a gold ring, my wedding ring, dotted with shiny stones and splendour. I try to lean forward more. There is no glass in the window frame of the car. I'm filled with warmth. The cloud looks icy but I'm not cold. I search again for the children, but they've gone. I see rust! The sparkly stones have turned into rust red diamonds, like the leaves that are turning from caramel to rust, sprinkling down, crumbling, and I have to catch the tiny stones, catch the falling leaves before they fritter and turn to dust and I grasp and all I touch is harsh rust.

I turn to Michael, but he is sleeping, oblivious to me and what's happening. There is no road on this journey, and he is asleep, and I can't reach out to touch him, to shake him awake. I look up, looking for stars but all I see are flying chuckle pink pigs, winged cherubs that smile and wink, babies on the wing. The pigs herd together in a gathering of silver halos, a prize porcelain collection; pigs, like the ones I collected when I was teenager. I fly with them when they call out to me and I'm swirling up, up, and up, hands outstretched. Then I reach up above and I'm no longer in the car.

I see Uncle Jack, his dead face staring at me from my grandmother's house. Old faces flash, a school-friend who was killed crossing the road, and she smiles a ghost's broken smile. I see my mother waving, a dozen colourful silk headscarves around her head. She's out of reach and she turns to go, waving at me and she is replaced by a young woman, dressed all in green. Even her face is green and her eyes glint emerald. She calls out names I can't hear, and she carries a flagon full of beer. I smile at her, I know her, she is the green lady looking for her children. I filter phantoms faces like a fast hand dealing a deck of cards. I search, looking for Tom, my husband Tom, but he isn't here. I can't find him, but the heat of stringed music warms me. I know it is he who is playing, high up in the Appalachian Mountains, playing for me. I close my eyes and hear him play so softly that my eyes fill with tears and I cry.

MICHAEL! I TRY to shout Michael to wake up and to listen to the music, but I can't speak. Diamond leaves float to me and pink chuckle pigs hold me and guide me down. I don't know where they're taking me, but I sense I'm safe.

I fall back into the soft smooth caramel leaf and slumber.

Sometime later I feel crisp fresh sheets on my back, and I fall, fall, fall back into them, soft, sleepy, tired. Someone calls my name. *Jane. Jane.* The whisper grows louder. *Jane!*

I open my eyes and a man in a white coat looks down at me, a bright light behind him.

He says, 'Welcome you back. We thought we'd lost you.'

'Wha...' I croak. It's hard to speak, my throat dry, raw, and sore.

'You were in a car accident. A lorry from the distillery met you head on, at the top of the bend. You were lucky.'

Lucky? How am I lucky? A familiar icy prickle runs down my back. I know what that means. *I'm lucky, others weren't* that's what *'you were lucky'* means. Then I hear the words, his words, *'always in my heart, Mum.'*

The hot tear runs down my face. I know I'm alive, my tears tell me it is so. I turn my head away from the doctor and look to my left.

There he is, standing tall and strong with blonde floppy hair in his eyes and a smile that has always comforted me. He reaches out to me and says, '*You we're always in my heart, Mum.*'

Playing with the House-Elves

Mother smelt of cookies and jasmine. Our busy family trampled carefree through her scrubbed floors and tidy kitchen. Her bosom was comforting in our many times of trouble. She soothed and gave us wise words when the world was falling apart.

When I became a mother, I marvelled at how she'd kept our house spit-spot.

House-elves, she'd laugh.

My heart breaks as I watch her wringing her hands in a corner of the home that cares for minds that are lost and bodies that are broken. We talk about pastimes and house-elves.

She says the house-elves came and took her.

Hedgehogs, Green Bottles, and Lilies

Everything was different on the day the hedgehogs failed to come. The silence provoked him, tantalising his senses. No rattling of chipped china plates, the absent prickly-backs no longer munching on softened bread and dog food, and the rain falling like his unshed tears; they were signs. It was time.

HE PICKED UP the racing-green bottle. It slotted easily into the usual spot in his hand, comfortable, like a well-worn glove. The stark white label showed its worth, a value of forty per cent, along with the government's warning that '*drinking may harm your health*.' The bottle was empty, not a drop of solace to soften the day. He was comforted by the familiarity in his hand and tried not to be dismayed by the lack of contents. He looked at the bottle, his reflection distorted with recognition of the colour of his hunger. The thick bevelled glass glistened with the aftereffects of neat gin, a reminder of the man that he was, the man that he had become; the man that he no longer wished to be.

I'm going to do it, remaking his promise, talking his way through it, the bottle is empty; I'm not going out for more. Farewell my lovely, my trusty companion.

He picked up his glass from the night before and opened up the dishwasher, clinking it against the others. He slammed the door, rattling the glass buddies. Howls of discontent were swished away by the glug and swirl of water rushing over the tumblers. He turned his back and he walked to another room, to another place, to another phase.

I can't go back. I can't. I made a promise. His shoulders dropped as he picked up a book, trying to read. *I made the promise. Again. This time. This time. The end.*

'*HEY, DAD! LOOK!* There's a hedgehog!' Bruce squealed, jumping up and down at the kitchen window.

'Don't be daft, son.' Tom rustled the newspaper, wondering if the yardarm was long enough yet, if it was a suitable time. Twenty minutes past two. Was that acceptable? Was it late enough? Somewhere the latitude would be right.

'Dad. Quick. Please! It might go in a minute. Come and look!'

A distraction. He could spare the time. It would fill up five minutes, put off the inevitable. The liquor sat patiently in the bottle on the windowsill, winking at him with the sun's reflection as he passed it by. Tom turned his back and walked over to Bruce, placing a hand on his son's shoulder. They looked outside. The wilderness waved at him in the light wind. He liked the overgrowth, the messy, in need of attention look, a reminder of his affinity with nature.

'There it is, Dad, over there,' Bruce whispered, child-like so the creature couldn't hear him. He pointed over to the left, near the dishevelled and rotting wooden shed.

The animal sniffed the ground around the burrow. Tom had filled it in three times, thinking it had been created by the local cats.

There it sat, looking at them, a proud prickled hedgehog.

NEVER NO MORE again. Life began and ended daily from the moment he took the first swig; arm in arm with his best friend, the bottle. Patience ran out on him, taking everyone with her. All had fallen by the wayside and he was alone. Without a slow rewind, only a dizzying fast forward, his solitary habit had become the way that it was. He liked the lonely comfort.

He opened the cellar door, tossed the empty bottle inside, another comrade for the green soldiers piled up, ready to be exiled to recycling centre. *If only I had the courage to be rid of them. And does one excuse that number of empties as a party?'* No party, just a very long wake.

He cringed at the crowd behind the door, remembering the pain, the money spent, the times that he forgot everything in his oblivion. The nights and days he didn't remember were countless, blessed relief and horrific totality of nothingness, but it was time, today, just like he knew it would be on the day that the hedgehogs didn't come.

'Next week, Dad, can we take some photos? I want to do my school project on Beattie.'

Bertie the hedgehog had become Beattie the day she brought her babies. Two tiny little creatures mewled alongside her, mooching for scraps and mother love.

'Of course, you can.' Tom ruffled his son's tousled head.

'Mum said we shouldn't encourage them. She said they have fleas.'

'Maybe we don't have to tell her,' Tom replied. *She's good at keeping secrets.*

'I'd like to be hedgehog, Dad. Then I can come and live here with you all the time.'

Tom mashed the pooch food, folding in the soaked bread, not looking at his son. 'It's right you live with your mum, Bruce. Everyone needs their mum.'

'I know but I could look after you if I lived here and I could see her every other weekend. She's got Gary and you don't have anyone. And anyway, you haven't got a mum.'

Tom bent level with Bruce and stared into his son's face. 'That's not your job, son. I'm a grown up, I don't need anyone to look after me.' He pulled his son towards him, held him close, and swallowed the lump in his throat as he wiped the back of his hand across his eyes.

'Mum said it's your own fault. She said that the bottle was your mistress and it's no wonder you're lonely. I heard her talking to Aunty Fizz on the telephone. She said that's why she was driven to Gary.'

'When you're older, son-'

'Yeah, yeah, I know. I'll understand then. It's not fair, Dad.'

Tom stood, looked out of the window, and cursed his ex-wife. Sandra had wanted out long before his drinking became more than a hobby. Tom knew about Gary. She hadn't let Tom anywhere near her for a long time, but he didn't want to leave. The more she left him home alone, the more the booze and he became buddies. In the end, it was easier to let her blame his drinking. In the end, it was easier to let her go.

'I could help you stop drinking, Dad. If you want to?'

Tom grabbed his son with an elbow around the neck and pulled him close into his body again.

'I promise I'll try, son. I won't let you down. It's just hard…but I promise…I'll try.'

The second wave of redundancy had him on the promised list. He wasn't an asset worth keeping. Too many days absent and when he did go to work, he wore too much aftershave and ate too many mints. They knew, and he knew they knew.

The only thing he wanted was to see his son. Those were the days he tried harder. *It was time for a change.*

IT WAS LESS than fifty yards from Tom's doorstep to their parked car. Sandra stood by her boyfriend's vehicle and Tom stood on his step, waving at Bruce. Somewhere in the middle, while Bruce's parents eyed each other, he disappeared.

They didn't see, but they both heard the crunch and smelt the acrid taste of scorched tyres on tarmac. They both ran.

He had no chance. It was sudden impact, unavoidable, nothing the driver could do. The small van hadn't been travelling fast but with both sides of the street filled with parked cars he hadn't seen the young boy's head bobbing along in line with the car rooftops. He hadn't seen his little body deviate from its straightforward path into the road.

They had no idea why he'd run, why he needed to cross the road, why he didn't continue down the street to his mother's waiting arms. Perhaps he saw something to distract him?

Tom cradled his dying son his arms and watched as Bruce's face paled with the approach of the sirens.

'The hedgehogs, Dad, the hedgehogs.'

And then he was gone.

THE PAIN, A physical spear of hurt that was there when he swallowed, that dug into his chest when he breathed, that pierced his stomach when he ate, was a constant – a grieving parent's heart, broken.

He walked, kidding himself it was exercise. He wandered the streets, looking, searching for his son. He saw a boy, then another. They all had remarkable faces, forgettable and unforgettable at the same time. In the end, they each had the same face. His face. It was always his face. Every child in every street, every park, every schoolyard, was Bruce.

But it wasn't. It never was and never would be. Tom's path would then lead him to the tinkle above the general dealer's door. Supplies; bread, milk, dog food, and gin.

Sometimes he'd add a little ham, sometimes a small chunk of cheese, but always the gin. The smooth green glass of home slipped neat, tight into the inside pocket of his jacket. His dependable anaesthetic would carry his body from grief to make the circus sing, to laugh at the dancing penguins and to help him to forget. For a while.

BRUCE WAS TEN yesterday. Would have been ten yesterday. There should have been a party with balloons, clowns, and little pretty girls with red ribbons in their hair. There should have been a lot of things.

Tom took lilies and laid them on the plinth. It was time, this time for real. He made a promise, the one he'd made to Bruce on the last day he'd spent with him. *I'm ready now, Son. It's time to let you go.*

Today the hedgehogs didn't come, and he knew why it was so. Oblivion belonged to yesterday. He and his trusty companion, they'd skipped their last fandango, sang their last refrain. And now he was ready to keep his promise to his son.

No more alcohol. No more pain. Perhaps pain, but a different kind, and no more booze. It was time to move on, like the hedgehogs. For Bruce.

Dancing with the Devil

Papa died when I was four and I wasn't to know him much. I remember a big man with a belly-laugh that shook our timbers. He'd get drunk some and then crash on the comfy chair and snore. I remember crawling on his knee and layin' my head upon his chest, letting his beery-breath wash over me as I snuggled into his bear-hug arms. He was soft as soft as she was hard as hard. Momma would haul my little body off my papa's belly and throw me to the floor.

'Git your bony lil' ass off up to ya own bed,' she'd spit and give a kick to my back as I scuttled away like a sewer rat caught chewing on the trash.

Some of Big Jo's men came and beat my papa for fornicating wiv' a woman called Jenni, but I dint' know what fornicating was, back when I was four. My momma let them in the house and all I saw of my papa after that was a big bloody mess on the floor. His legs were bent in a way like what legs aren't supposed to go. His face was mashed potato and he had more blood on the floor than I knew a man had in his body. My momma telt me I had to say goodbye to papa and kicked me out to play. When I came back from my play, papa was gorn.

Momma said, 'Chile, yo papa is dead.'

The floor had been scrubbed and all that was left of papa was a big pink stain on the floorboards like the big pink stain he left on my life.

Momma shacked up with Billy-Boy pretty soon after that so I'sa guessing he was on the scene before papa was gorn. Not that she woulda telt ya that.

I wasn't keen on Billy-Boy but he didn't do me no wrong so I just lived my own life and kept outta Momma's way. She was handy with a slap and that sharp tongue of hers so I did the housework when she telt' me and skipped off orn out afterwards. If it wasn't up to 'her stannards' I'd get it. Standards. Ha. She had no standards hersel' 'cos she was a simple scrubber lady who made her living on her back and let her daughter to do the real scrubbing in the house.

She was no lady, neither. Every day she had me scrub that pink stain some, on account that one day I'd scrub the old man outta her life.

You can tell I don't like my momma none.

Papa had been dead eleven long years. Billy-boy had been around more than my own papa and s'long as he got his booze, he was dandy. Until she pimped me to him.

She tried for babies wiv' Billy-boy but lost two and couldn't fall again so she hatched hersel' a plan.

She said to me, 'Now, Chile, now yor a woman wiv' ya bleedin, it's yor turn.'

Like I said, I din't like nor mind Billy-Boy so much before but I didn't fancy him none. He was forty, fat, and sweaty. I was fifteen and dint' wanna be fornicating wiv' anyone. And I definitely dint' want no babbies.

She put the blues on the old wireless and gave me a glass of vinger vino.

'To relax ya, gal,' she said, with that spiky look in her eye.

I knew it was to get me drunk but there was her, him, and me, and no escape. So, I drank. And then some more.

I needed that drink. I needed to be drunk for what Momma had in mind for me.

She played him too, dressing hersel' up all fancy in lacy stockings and flashy, floaty silky stuff. Then she told him to get his ass on up and dance. He'd had a few beers an' so had she, afore we crashed onto the floor, a jumble of arms and legs, right on papa's pink stain.

The next weekend she plied me some more and cosied hersel' up to old Billy-boy right in front of my eyes. She called it my 'education' and she showed me how to make a man happy. He was game on, sitting there while she worked her voo-doo magic on his man-piece. I watched, never seen those sorts of things in my life afore. I din't know of carrying-ons like it and all that sexy stuff made me blush red raw. She played it well, introdoocin' me to the ways o' the woman.

The weekend after that she telt' me to dance with him, her Billy-boy. She gave me brassieres, stockings, and vino, and she made my face up with full on red lips an' all. She even splashed me wiv' her best sweet-smelling perfoom and laughed when it made me gag some. She put the slow sexy music on to play, just like she knew Billy-

Boy liked. He licked his lips when he looked at me and we both knew he was up for it.

And so, I had to dance with the devil and all that she meant.

IT WASN'T LONG afore I fell. My momma loved me then. Gave me everything a girl could want if she had a momma who really loved her. And I didn't have to have no more Billy-boy. He was all hers and I wasn't to be touching him agin. Didn't stop him wanting a bit of young ass flesh though 'cos he still kept comin' back for sweet meat. I dint' mind too much 'cos he called me 'preeetty' and hugged me like I'd not been hugged before. He even said he loved me, and I thought that was kinda cute and I'd a gotten used to a man by then and it was her own fault for makin' me do it the first time.

My baby's due just after ma sixteenth birthday and then I'm a gorn. I ain't stickin' around none. Papa's pink stain on the floor is gettin' less and less and I don't wanna go forgettin' him any. I don't wanna be around for the baby none either. Momma tole everyone I was a whore-girl for bringing trouble to yon door so they y'all give me the looks and call me a honky-whore.

I've got me a plan. Papa's been a talkin' to me at night when I'm alone in my bed. I never thought I'd hear from him agin. I'm a gonna join my papa 'cos he the only one who loved me for proper. I'm a gonna carve Billy-Boy's name on my heart and make my own big stain on Momma's floor mysel'. Somethin' to do with fornicating, just like papa. And she can keep my baba and look at the stains on the floor and the stains in her cold heart and remember some. It's all her fault 'cos she wanted me to have her baba for her. I din't have no choice. She made me do it.

She go on an' made me dance with the devil.

Need to Talk to You

Della heard those fatal words, '*I need to talk to you*'. A cold trickle made its way through her veins.

From childhood when her father beckoned, or the schoolteacher glanced over half-moon spectacles, or the vicar called deep from within his starched-white dog collar, she'd shudder and fear the words as her world crumbled. '*I need to talk to you.*'

Her father would disguise his lined face with a smile, but she knew. His dry humour, mocking her, making fun of her, filling her with his scorn and sarcasm and bitter hollow words, all proved how little she meant to him and how much she was his burden. As she learnt not to trust him and to move away from his sour underarm hugs, it taught her not to trust anyone. Least of all the mother who left her with this man when she died a death her father could never get over. A death he blamed Della for because without her, his unwanted daughter, his darling wife would never have died. It was Della's fault. Always Della's fault. She tried to trust her first boyfriend, Malcolm, he with a blonde flick for a fringe and eyes the colour of melted chocolate. She remembered how he said, '*I want to show you something*,' as he took her over the stile and up to the old barn at the back of Blackstock's fields. Della thought she'd hear the wonderful words of love but he didn't talk to her at all as he made her take off her pants and forced her to lay on the cool damp straw that prickled the tops of her legs. He didn't speak as he forced himself into her. He made sure she didn't speak because he clamped his gruff hand with fingers like sausages right over her mouth so she could do nothing but keep her silence. After the deed was done and a trickle of warm blood weaved its way down her leg, he said, '*I need to talk to you.*'

Her stomach turned, making everything inside turn and tumble like an opened bag of ice cubes.

He said, 'You were rubbish. It was rubbish. But you're good enough to practice on so come back on Saturday.' He ignored the trickle down her leg just like he ignored the trickle down her red ruddy cheeks. 'And if you tell anyone I'll say you made me do it. I'll tell them you're a slag.' He dug his blunt fingernails into her skinny forearm. 'Gettit? Get it?'

Della nodded, eyes down, seeing a field full of green sparkles of grass as she tried to stop him seeing how wet her eyes were. She reached out her other hand to his, but he slapped it away.

'You're history. It's over. I'm with Sylvie now. But like I just said, you're good enough to practice on. Just make sure you're here five o'clock on Saturday. Don't be late. Right?'

She didn't know what to say, so she said nothing but the ice-cold fear inside her made her turn up for the following three Saturdays until he said he didn't need her anymore, he had practised enough.

HER TEACHER, MRS Hetheringstone, who looked like a stork and taught her confusing maths, said to her one day after lunch, '*I need to talk to you.*'

Della felt her face flop in the hang-dog style she'd become accustomed to, her eyes searching the scuffed classroom lino. 'Stay back after break. I'll see you then,' the Stork sneered. Della had a fleeting thought she may have been picked for prize-giving. Or maybe the teacher thought she should audition for the play after school. Della loved being the maid in the last school production. She only had three lines and thought she read well but when she took a week off school because of tonsillitis, they picked Carol Marshall to take her part instead and she never got it back. Maybe, perhaps, they would let her have another chance and The Stork was going to tell her she could be in the next play.

'Look at this work! Shoddy. Lazy. Messy. And wrong. So very wrong. You haven't been trying at all, have you?' The Stork spat and glared at her with eyes that popped out from her head, as though they were on stalks, too.

'But Miss …'

'Don't you *but Miss* me, young lady. This is totally unacceptable. You'll be in Mr Brown's class from now on. The remedial class. There's no room for you here.'

Della was dismissed even though it wasn't her work. It was Nora Bacon's maths book, but Nora Bacon was off school with a broken wrist. No doubt the Stork would have realised later but Della knew the teacher hated her, didn't like her at all, and wouldn't listen, anyway. Della attended Mr Brown's class and she passed her O level at C grade. Della knew she'd never have managed that in the Stork's class.

When the vicar told Della he needed to talk to her, she thought it might have been her chance to be a bearer, to carry the precious wafer tray, or to give out the wine on Easter Sunday. Perhaps, he might even allow her to say a reading? She fantasised it was Daniel 5:27, her favourite. *I was found wanting …*

But it was nothing like that. As Della picked at the dull patchwork cloth on the front pew and sat looking at Father Clark, her stomach catapulted the ice-cold fear of tumbling ice cubes once more.

'I really think you should reconsider your place in the choir, Della. You're an … err … erm … an *enthusiastic* singer … but there are those who sing better,' he said. He suggested she may have some coaching lessons before rejoining. He patted her on the shoulder and added a patronising 'bless you my child'. Della looked at the tall white candles flickering, the burning light glinted off the stained-glass window and blurred. She looked at Jesus hanging from the cross with his head down, bleeding from the thorns in his crown and not for the first time, she felt his despair. Jesus. She felt such pain.

ANOTHER KNOCK, ANOTHER dent, another let down. Always the same. *I need to talk to you.* Maybe, she thought, it was because she had no mother to protect her, no female influence in her life. She knew she was plain Jane, a victim some might say, someone others could hate without thinking too much about, someone to kick when they were down, someone easy to dismiss, or hang their bad feelings on like a redundant coat peg, forgotten and ignored. She tried to be optimistic, to not hate too much, but couldn't help to search for what it was about her that made people dislike her so.

She tried hard to reinvent herself. She took a job in the city, started at the bottom as a tea-girl, despite a clutch of credible O levels. She progressed to office cleaner, then postal clerk, and found herself a position as office junior. When Della made it to second typist, she rented a flat nearer to where she worked. She adored her little home and kept it spotless. She took some classes to build up self-confidence and self-esteem. She tried hard to forget, but it was often easier to remember.

Then Della met a man, a kind man, a quiet man, and he opened up to her like a book that contained excitement and escapism and some of the love she'd never had. Della adored him. Brian was Someone Like Her. And for the first time her world had warmth and love and passion.

Della and Brian had been married for eight months and six days when he called her at work. He uttered the words, '*I need to talk to you.*'

THE SPEAR OF fear was more than a bank of tumbling ice cubes. It ran down to her toes. The light she'd carried with her since meeting Brian extinguished in an instant when he spoke those words.

Della arrived home at five minutes past five o'clock. She had stopped off to buy chicken, peppers, and rice. She made dinner as usual and sat at the table, waiting for him.

She heard his key in the lock. Listened to the turn of the latch. The squeak of the door. Her face flushed, red hot. He was home.

Brian looked happy, smiley, relaxed, as he kissed her cheek. He poured himself a cup of tea from the ready pot. She rose from the table, took his coat, and hung it up. He

117

stood by the kitchen counter, slurping and slopping his tea with a stupid grin on his face.

Della opened the drawer beneath the kettle.

He started to speak, 'I need to talk to you.' He paused, then said, 'I really think …'

She picked up the first thing she touched. She spun. Turned around fast, bread knife clutched tight her hand. She looked at it. Looked at him. She saw his glistening blue eyes the colour of the sapphire in her engagement ring. She moved forward a fairy footstep and tightened her fingers around the handle, moulding it to her grip. She stepped forward another fairy footstep.

His brow creased. 'Wha …'

She lunged, dug the knife into his midriff. Once. Then out again. And in again. And out. And she didn't stop in-and-out, in-and-out until she saw the first sign of blood oozing from his mouth and the gush of red from his belly covered her hand like a glove.

He tried to speak, 'Family … baby … time …' his eyes pleaded with hers.

In that moment, between his last word and his last breath, she knew she'd made a terrible mistake. A gargantuan mistake.

He thought it was time they should start a family.

She hadn't given him the chance. She had learnt not to believe despite the heat, the passion, the beauty in him, and the life he'd shown her could exist if only she could trust.

Her screams continued to ring out, a constant screech, until the neighbours rang the police. Della was taken away from the flat smeared in her husband's blood and handcuffed, wrists bound together.

The police tried to ascertain what had happened. She blubbed and burbled and cried. She rambled about someone called Daniel and they were confused as her husband was Brian. She uttered over and over again for more than an hour '*I was found wanting*'. And then she fell silent, refusing to speak.

When the detective came to the cell said, '*It's time. We need to talk to you*,' she screamed forever more.

Forever Day

I know he had a one-night stand once. Sort of.

He sat at the end of our bed, his head in his hands, and began to confess. 'It was the summer holidays…when Mum came to stay.'

Living abroad meant she never had to be a hands-on grandma. It must have meant a lot to her, giving up her Spanish summer. I have to give her credit though, after I left, she stayed for over a month.

'She made me go out…said I needed a bit of fun.' His hands trembled. '*You know* how I hate town centre drinking.'

It never was his scene.

'I saw Trish…she asked me about you.'

I liked Trish.

'And…and she was kind to me,' he whispered. 'We had a few drinks…she made me laugh…made me forget. For a little while.'

It hurt, when he said that, but I was being unreasonable.

'She asked me back for coffee…I thought that's what she meant.' He hollow-laughed. 'Just for coffee…'

I smiled. The buffoon. He would think that. I had the urge to ruffle his thick unruly hair.

'I ended up in her bed.'

Whoa – too much detail. 'I couldn't do it.' A big fat tear fell onto to the floor and disappeared into the carpet. 'I wasn't drunk…I just…I didn't want to. It felt like I was being unfaithful.' The muffled words choked in his throat. 'I told her…told her I was still in love with you.'

I wished I could hug him, wrap myself around him but I couldn't.

'I don't *want* anyone else. I want you! I *need* you,' he begged. 'We *all* need you.' He cried – for me, for him, for the kids, for our life that was meant to be. He looked up into the dark, his heart breaking mine again, 'I promised you there would be nobody else!'

'LOOK AT THE state of their hair! Is that supposed to be a plait? Does he think that's a parting?' I call out, angry with the world, with everyone and everything.

The time I'd spent showing Dave how to do a neat hairstyle and the kids still go to school with 'Daddy hair'. I'd stocked the cupboards with super strong hairspray but the only one using it is Little David. He stands in front of the mirror, tweaking his strands every which way.

'When did you become so fashion conscious, Davey?' I laugh but he doesn't hear.

I look at them, Mary, Little David, and Melissa, our pretty young children. I ache with the love. Mary, fine at eleven, and Little David, such a tall boy for ten; they seem so grown up. Our little Melissa is not so little now that she's eight. Such an imp! With my face and her father's sense of humour, she's lucky; it could have been the other way round.

I cry in desperate silence. I know he's doing a good job; the best he can. He's struggling, like I knew he would. He begged me not to go but in the end, I had no choice. It was awful, the kids seeing us like that. It was a relief, of sorts. I'd hoped Dave would find somebody else in time, but it's been almost a year.

'You need someone, Dave,' I'd told him. 'So do the kids.'

'There's no one else for me, you know that.' His eyes were flat.

'Don't be so stupid.' I laughed, and though I could see his hurt, what could I do? I was going and there was nothing anyone could do that would stop me.

'*You* are their mother!' His finger, too sharp, jabbed me in the chest.

I had no answer for him as we held one another tight.

'I CAN SMELL Mum!' Little David shouted from the hallway.

Mary gave him a dig in the midriff.

'Ouch!' He yelped.

'Shut up!' she hissed at him.

'Wha'd you hurt me for?' Little David rubbed his tummy, exaggerating like he usually did.

'I don't want to upset Dad,' said Mary, scowling at her brother.

'He's in the car.' He pointed outside.

I bend to kiss our children on top of their heads as they prepare to leave the house. Shoes, coats, and bags are scattered all over house. I smile. Some things don't change. I want to call out, tell them I'm here, watching, and to behave themselves.

'I sprayed some of her perfume.' Mary's eyes are bright with sweet tears as she confesses.

'I'm telling!' Melissa, bless her, she doesn't understand.

'Squeak! You better not tell.' Mary jabbed her little sister in the ribs.

If only I could come back…but I can't.

'It's Mum's birthday and I want her to be with me today.' Mary's voice broke.

'Now, children! That's enough. Daddy's waiting.' I try to usher them out, but they can't hear as I shout, 'Have a good day!'

Mary looks back at the house and I see her mouth, 'I love you.'

I wave and reply, 'I love you too,' but she can't see me.

I should go, but I can't; I'm stuck. They sense it too. Mary sometimes sneaks into the back bedroom. They call it Mummy's room. It will always be my room, the room where I could tell them how much I loved them and how

I'll always be in their hearts, the room where I had the chance to say goodbye.

Dave lay with me that last night, hugging me as I took my last breath. I watched the children kiss me goodbye the following morning. I watch now as they go about their day and wish I could be their mother again.

I need to be here today, and then I have to leave, to let them be. It's hard to leave my family but I need to go so they can move on, and they can't with me stuck here.

Today, on my birthday, I would be thirty-five. It is an age I will ever be.

Time Enough

She's ready, by the door, waiting. So is he. She doesn't move, eyes shut tight, glued together and defiant. It's stalemate.

He tugs at his starched shirt collar and checks his pearlescent cufflinks, encased in silver. They belonged to his father, an inheritance. Worn at the wedding, every wedding, and will be passed down to his only son.

He waits some more. She doesn't move.

'Ready, Mother?' he asks, remembering yesteryear when she'd stand on the doorstep, looking out for him, waiting for him to return home.

She doesn't answer. Her face stony, lips clamped. She doesn't want to leave yet.

Time ticks by on the clock on the wall. It belongs to another era, another age. Keeping time on the past. The loud clack as the minute hand passes time is a reminder that it's nearly over. About to be done. For what is now to be received, for the last time. After today, like many other things in the little house on the left, before the grocer's, it will no longer be needed. Bundled off to the thrift shop, into a crowded charity bag, to another home, or consigned to the bin where it might be left, unwanted, not needed, a cheap encumbrance that's taking up space on a shelf.

He waits. She doesn't move, she isn't leaving. It's her home.

Then the engine rattle stops outside the front door. Black-suited, polished-shoed, sombre-faced men enter the little house.

'Ready?' says the one in the top hat. But this is no mad-hatters tea party.

He nods, eyes bright with sparkle, and he tugs his shirt sleeves once more. His hands brush back his hair, and he whispers, 'Goodbye.' It's for her. For him. For them both.

Top-hat man closes the lid on the past. They pick her up, six sad strong men. He, her son, stands at the back. The casket is heavy in contrast to her light frame. She is held inside now, no release, a dark prison, forever her home.

It's time.

A solitary tear tracks a silent goodbye.

She must now leave, for the last time.

She Forgot All About Mikey

D on't blame my mother. Please don't blame her. It's not her fault, it's really not. It's just the way I am. And we can't help being what we are, can we? We're just a little different is all, me and Mikey.

MY BIG SISTER, Pauline, died when I was young. Too young, because I don't remember her. I have floating memories of a heavy cloud that was full of tears as it hung in the kitchen and in my mother's bedroom. I sometimes heard my mother howling and she had other types of crying too. Her cry-crying was all the time at that time, howling and otherwise. I've forgotten the times when she didn't cry or howl or whimper like a little creature lost and alone. But she wasn't alone. She had me. She always had me.

And there was a man. I remember a man, tall and big but not so strong because he cried too. And he had my face. Or I had his. Then he left and I only saw him when I looked in the mirror. It was only then that I remembered him. That's all I have, some vague memories of my face being his face and perhaps because we have the same face that's part of the reason why she did it. She did it all to help her forget. And she did it all to help her remember. She forgot me and she forgot my father and all she ever remembered was Pauline.

I have images of my sister that flit into my memory from time to time but I know they're really images from the worn photographs hidden in the back of the store cupboard under the stairs in a battered old-fashioned suitcase that smells of frogs and dead flowers from the pond where Pauline drowned. Or maybe it doesn't but I like to think I can smell the fat green frogs on the suitcase whenever I sneaky-peak a look to remind myself of my sister. I remember her from our mother's memories too, when she talks of Pauline, her only daughter. I remember her also because of the things I've learnt about her by knowing her in other ways. Like wearing her clothes and growing my hair like she had hers, all blonde and curly and pretty. Like living the life that was supposed to be hers.

And forgetting about Mikey.

BY THE TIME I was four, mother had taken to calling me Paulie. Little Paulie. Only I wasn't Paulie, little or otherwise. I was Mikey. All Mikey. But she forgot about him.

Before I started school, we moved house. It was just me and her because the man with my face had long left us. We moved two hundred miles away from the garden pond full of fat green frogs and dead flowers where Pauline died.

Mother told everyone I was Paulie and everyone had to call me that name.

'Hello Paulie,' said my teacher as she shook my hand. She always called me Paulie and I didn't tell her I wasn't Paulie but Mikey, he who had been forgotten. Mother wouldn't like that. She wouldn't like me correcting anyone about my name.

Everyone thought I was a girl. I played with girls and kept away from rough boys who played at being cowboys and Red Indians, or bank robbers and policemen, or footballers and racing car drivers. I had little golden curls and tiny painted fingernails and long flutter-by eyelashes that ladies said they envied. I looked like a girl, acted like a girl, and began to think I was a girl. I didn't realise I was any different. Not then.

Mother taught me to sit down to do my business on the toilet and she bought me pretty panties with daisies embroidered on the front. Daisies reminded me of Pauline. Daisy chains hanging from her hair, from her neck, and in her fingers. They loved her, they loved her not. Mother taught me to tuck my tail away and keep it hidden in the daisy pants. It mustn't ever come out and I must never talk of it. She would warn me with the tip of a finger to her lips, hiding her smoky breath that was rich and sour. I didn't know that other little girls didn't have pee-pee tails, but I knew I must never talk about private things so it didn't matter if they did or if they didn't. When there was a boy I quite liked and I wanted to be his friend, I didn't know any different and neither did he. We were far too young for any of that sort of stuff.

Mother took me to a dance class. I became very good. I liked ballet but preferred tap and jazz and I won gold medals and certificates with my name on, Paulie Harris.

Nobody suspected. Not then. Not ever. And everyone loved Paulie because Paulie had that something different. Even I forgot about Mikey when I danced.

She read me fairy tale stories with princesses and handsome princes that I acted out in the upstairs attic room where I played on my own. I loved being on stage, acting and singing and smelling the pancake face make-up, the thick liquorice block mascara, the rich ruby lipstick, and the stinging starchy hairspray. Mother loved dressing me in frills and flounce. I'd always preferred pink. And sparkles. And silver. And all that glitters, gold or not. I can't say my preferences are her fault, because I don't remember a time when I thought differently.

She didn't let me join the cub scouts and neither did she let me join the brownies. 'I can't have you going away camping in tents, Paulie. You're different to the other children. You're special.'

I knew I was special. I knew I was different. By the time I realised how different, I couldn't say anything. What *could* I say?

Why did you dress me in my dead sister's clothes?

Why did you grow my hair out from the short back and sides style that the man with my face wore?

Why did you put my golden hair in rags at night to make it all curly and pretty?

Why did you teach me to play with dolls and not cars and guns like the other boys I went to school with?

Why did you make me believe I was a girl?

And why did you give me her name and forget all about Mikey?

MOTHER LOVED ME. I know that. She loved her little Paulie. She loved my sister, Pauline. But she hated men. All men. So you can see – it's not my fault. And it's not her fault. It's just the way we're wired.

Don't blame her. I don't. It's not her fault that I lost my temper and smashed the back of her head in with heel of a diamante dance shoe. Sixty times and more, like Lizzie Borden who had an axe and gave her mother forty whacks. Or it might have been only ten, I don't know. Some things I just don't remember.

I put mother's body in the attic room and propped her up at the window with her long blonde hair streaked with red strands, all hanging down in a sweep after I'd brushed it one hundred times and I left her there, waiting, looking out for her prince to come like Rapunzel or

Sleeping Beauty who had to wait one hundred years. She's there, watching and waiting for him to come and it might be the man with my face. He might come back to rescue her, and to rescue me. Or maybe he won't.

Please don't blame my mother. She forgot. That is all. She forgot about Mikey. She forgot about me grieving for my little big sister. She forgot about growing up. She had forgotten I would grow. Grow strong and grow like a man with hairs in all the strange girl places – on my chest, and up my legs, and on my chinny-chin-chin and she never thought about when the daisy pants wouldn't fit anymore, no matter how hard I tried to strap myself down. She forgot how I would grow. That's all.

Why do you ask why I did it? Yesterday I heard the doctor who gives me the purple and pink pills say that the build up of testosterone was to blame, along with a lifetime of confusion.

And it was no wonder the elastic snapped. And I thought about the elastic snapping on my daisy pants.

Don't blame Paulie. Don't blame her. Don't blame me. It's just the way we're wired. It was Mikey that did it. Because mother forgot all about him and he didn't like that.

Mind the Gap

The same dream, the same words, every time. The rumble of the train, the shake of the bed, both imaginary, but the start of the nightmare that signalled the worst would follow. It never deviated and she could never stop it. Relentless, it flew into the tunnel without stopping. She could smell the musty dank air and could hear the scurry of the track mice. Litter flew up and around in a fanfare, preparing for the train to come to a halt in the station, but it never did stop.

She was desperate to call out a warning, to scream out, but she was impotent, unable to tell him. Then it was too late and once more she'd wake up shouting 'mind the gap, mind the gap'.

WHEN HE WAS first born, she had the dream once in a while. The older he became, the more it happened. She made sure they never went on the Tube and moved out of London when he was five years old. It made her feel safe.

When he was eighteen and came home with an offer of a job in London. She told him no, he couldn't go.

'Because of a stupid dream? Mother!'

'Please, son, please don't go.'

'It's good money. I can't turn it down. Besides, I want to go.'

She could do nothing to stop him. Time passed, and she still she dreamt. The turned twenty. Then thirty. Over time they laughed, and the Tube tension eased, but she never forgot.

IT WAS THE evening of his fortieth birthday. The phone rang just after midnight and she knew. When they told her he'd been pushed, there was nothing he could do. Drunken students having a prank bumped into him and he fell.

'It was Holborn, wasn't it?'

They put it down to mother's intuition, not understanding her dream.

SHE STANDS ON the platform of Holborn Tube station,

waiting for the last train to arrive, watching the track mice, feeling the hot gust of wind buffer her as the train approached, the litter flying up in a fanfare, and as it screeched into the station, she jumped.

The Piano Man's Daughter

When I went looking for my mother, it took me three years to find the policewoman who could help me. I was twenty-one when I found her. I also found the truth.

I was twenty-one years too late.

I'D ALWAYS KNOWN I was adopted. My parents told me when I was young, and I don't remember a time I didn't know that my mum and dad weren't my real mum and dad. I knew nothing about my heritage and the older I became, the more I began to think about it and the more it haunted me.

It wasn't that I didn't like my life, my advantages – I did. I just had this twisting, burning need inside me to find out where my thick black hair, my green-grass eyes, and my flat feet came from. I was happy, flighty, and had a great wicked humour that my adoptive family lacked. I had everything I could ever want, but I didn't know me.

When I was sixteen, I asked for some information. My parents told me what I already knew – that I'd been adopted by them in October 1989 through Westminster social services and they gave me my name – Angelina. That's all they said they could tell me. It wasn't like it is today. I had no life-book or historical records to accompany me. I imagined myself as a lost puppy, free to a good home, kind owners required.

I was placed with the Cuthbertson's and they gave me everything they could. Dad was in banking and Mum was a PA somewhere in Whitehall. I was educated in the best private day school and we took fantastic holidays abroad every year. I had a private allowance and access to credit accounts at the top West End boutiques.

I didn't realise, nor appreciate, the privilege because my friends all had the same, yet I still felt like an outsider and I can't blame anybody for that but myself. I just didn't seem to fit.

I was eighteen when I decided to do some investigating.

I SAT IN the offices of Pimlico Social Services with the smell of dust, dirt, and old files. A tall black guy with dreadlocks was banging on the reception desk and demanding someone let him see his kids. He smelt sweet, a mix of coconut and hash. I shrank into my plastic bucket-chair as he flounced down beside me, thick twisted noodle hair flying. The waft of dirty stale alcohol landed with a whack that hit my stomach like I'd been punched. Thankfully, a large lady with a musty smell of her own called my name. She stood at the security door, barring access to all information and told me to come back later that afternoon. She thrust a card at me with her name and office phone number – Margaret Baker, social worker.

I returned at two o'clock. The black guy had gone and in his place was an oriental family jabbering away in what I assumed was mandarin. I swallowed uncomfortably as I watched the family struggle to make themselves understood to the lady behind the counter. The littlest boy started to cry and clung to his mother's long skirt. I smelt the urine as it pooled by his feet and seeped into his little open-toed sandals.

I felt out of place with my heels, my made-up face, and passport to riches. I eyed the family in front of me and I wondered, was this what I'd come from? A family who couldn't hope to care for me? A family who loved me so much they didn't want me to grow up as they had, needy and neglected by a society that made it hard for them to cope? A family who could offer me love but nothing else? I fantasised about how I could make it all right for my original family now that I had money of my own. I could repay them with love, kindness, and the sorts of luxuries I'd grown up with. I could prove to them that I'd made it, that they'd done the right thing for me and it was time for me to come home.

Margaret called me forward and took me into a dingy airless room. I saw a file on the desk. It didn't look very thick.

'Does your mother know you've come here, Angelina?' She asked.

'I've come here to find my mother,' I said, not understanding the question.

'I mean your adoptive mother,' she said.

'Err...no.' I swallowed, my mouth dry. 'I've talked about it with her, but she doesn't know I've come today.

Do I have to tell her?' I hoped not. I wasn't sure she'd understand.

'No. You're eighteen but we always suggest you talk it through first. Have you had any counselling?'

'No. Do I have to?' I didn't want counselling. I just wanted to find my mother. And then, hopefully, my father. Maybe a sibling, or two.

'No, but there are many reasons why children are adopted, and we suggest they have counselling when looking for their birth family. It's not an easy process and it's not all happy endings.'

She smiled at me. I half-smiled back, unsure. What could be so difficult?

I'D BEEN given to social services for adoption by the maternity ward of St Thomas's Hospital. That's all I knew. There was a report by a policewoman, shoulder-number 821CV, with a scrawled signature and the surname WATSON. She said 'adoption' to the courts after all police enquiries to trace relatives had come to nothing. There were plenty of reports and orders in my file, but they were all about the court process and nothing about my birth parents.

Margaret said, 'Apparently, the paperwork had been with the police and as the years went by, when we tried to get it back, it was lost in the system.' She explained that back then, the turnover of staff was high, people moved on, offices relocated, and it was easy get lost in an overloaded system.

Like many, I was a casualty of 'the system'. There was nobody left from that era who could tell me anything. The hospital couldn't, or wouldn't, help, so I decided to find the policewoman. They have to tell you the truth, don't they? The police.

I told my mum and she said she'd help me. She was a little hurt, didn't understand my desperate need, but as ever, she supported me, and I loved her all the more for it. I think she thought that once I'd found what I was looking for, things would settle and go back to normal, a quiet little life in the middle-class privileged existence that they'd provided for me. Mum was nearly sixty and I realised my birth mother might be half her age.

I realised she might be worried. I told her, 'I'll be lucky. I'll have two Mums, Mum!'

I FOUND OUT quite quickly that CV meant Vine Street. However, Vine Street Police Station had long been converted to offices and everything was now located at West End Central Police Station. Then I found out that my officer, 821CV, had transferred to Chingford in 1992 to work in a sort of child protection/vulnerable persons team. So, I went to Chingford.

821CV was now 621JC and then she married, had a baby, then another. Then she left.

Sergeant Taylor told me that Diane Watson had married a friend of a friend of hers called Steve Ash, who was also a policeman. 'They went somewhere up north. To a constabulary force,' she said.

'Do you know where?' I asked, elated at the breakthrough.

'The connections were loose in 1996 when they moved so she could be anywhere. Sorry. That's all I know. I don't suppose I should be telling you this but if you find her, say 'Hi' from me.'

As I left, she wished me luck.

I began to feel as if Diane was my mother. I was obsessed with finding her. I couldn't concentrate on anything else. I took a gap year. I fantasised about what I would say when I found her. I fantasised what I would say when I then found my mother.

Up north was a big place. I spent a fortune on phone calls to various police headquarters dotted on the map above Watford. They either didn't know or wouldn't say and couldn't help. I spent hours browsing the Internet. One day, after various sites full of useless information, I found a press report from 2003. Detective Sergeant Diane Ash had identified the body of a man accused of abusing his stepdaughter after he had been found hanging in his Newcastle bail-address flat. I rang Northumbria Police Headquarters. They didn't have any officers called Ash. When I mentioned the newspaper article, they suggested I tried Durham.

Bingo! Yes, they had officers Stephen and Diane Ash on their register. But euphoria crashed to despair when the polite lady on the other end of the phone told me they'd both retired from the force. No, she couldn't give me their address. No, she had no further information. Sorry.

I cried for a week. It was more than an obsession. I tried the social network sites – Friends Reunited, Facebook, Twitter, MySpace – but I realised that I had no idea what Diane Ash looked like, how old she was or even if she'd speak to me. I'd all but given up when I was idly googling. I wasn't expecting to turn up anything new and I almost missed it. Dinah Ash – a writer from Crieff, Scotland, had a poem published on a website. I clicked the link.

It was a poem about waiting and about there being no end, not yet. It spoke to me. I knew it was her. Dinah – Diane. Writers sometimes use different names, didn't they? I read the poem, over and again. *There is no end, not yet…*

There was an email address. I tapped out a message. I deleted it and started again. I clicked send. I told her I liked her poem and that it resonated with me. Was she the same person who had worked at Chingford with Sgt Taylor? If so, she said to say 'hi'.

Was it too much? Not enough?

A week later I received a reply.

Hi. Thank you for your message. I appreciate your comments about my poem. Please tell Sgt Taylor I said Hi back. Kind regards, Dinah. (You can find more of my work at writersright.com)

I researched her work and found poems and stories littered with police references. I googled images and found a grainy picture of Dinah in The Courier. She looked younger than I thought she would be. In her forties, long dark hair, nice smile with kind eyes. There was only one thing left to do. Go to Crieff.

Mum came with me. We booked a bed-and-breakfast and left the leaving date open.

First stop, the police station. No. They did not give out ex-cops addresses even if they knew where they lived. A young sergeant looked at me with suspicious eyes and when he asked for my details, I guess he thought I might be an ex-con looking for revenge. I gave him my name and address just in case he passed it on to her.

Next stop, the library. Writers hang out there, don't they? The librarian was giving nothing away either. She offered me a visitor's card if I wanted to book out her latest anthology, but I wanted the woman, not her work.

I went for a coffee. Writers wrote in coffee houses, didn't they?

On the fourth day I finally found her thanks to a loose-lipped shop keeper. Turning up on a stranger's doorstep looking for information was what Diane had done for years. Now it was my turn.

When I found her, I didn't know what to say. The sob caught in the back of my throat. When I said I'd been looking for her for the last three years, she ushered me inside and fed me sugary tea. I have no idea what she must have been thinking. She was kind. Very kind and looked so…so…ordinary… so mumsy in a mid-life kind of way; not young, not old, just kind and warm and sort of nice.

In between broken sobs and digestives, I told her my story, what I knew of it, and after some persuasion that yes, I was ready, yes, I needed to know, yes, it was the right thing to do, then, after all that, it was her turn to tell me what she knew.

She, my mother, was called Angela. Angie. A Scottish woman, little and fiery with funny tongue and a sad life. She lived on the streets with the vagrants, a down-and-out. She told everyone she was a piano man's daughter. Diane knew nothing of her previous life, how she came to be on the streets, nothing. Angie had short cropped black hair with matching black eyes and was a drinker She drank anything she could get, just like the people she shared her life with did.

Diane smiled and said, 'I was a kind copper, one of those who would nick the street people in bad weather, so they had a warm bed and bellyful of breakfast the next morning. Otherwise, we left them alone, unless they'd done something they shouldn't, like fight in the street, or threaten someone.'

I said, 'Thank you,' on behalf of a mother I didn't know.

'People end up on the streets for all sorts of reasons. Angie had a thing for a guy called Miles. He'd been a professional golfer, apparently, but lost the lot to gambling and drink. Angie fell pregnant and told everyone this was her chance of a proper life. She said Miles was the father of her baby and they were going to set up home together, be like normal people. I hoped that was true but...'

Then Diane took my hands and I saw a tear sparkle in her as she looked at me. 'I don't want to hurt you but if you want the truth, if you need to know the truth, then I can tell you.'

My heart was fluttering, my head pounding. Yes, I needed to know.

'That's okay,' my voice cracked. 'Please...just tell me.'

'Angie slept with men on the street, but only the guys like her, the homeless and the down and outs, in return for a can of special brew, or some drugs. It'd helped take the pain away. That was life on the street. Who knew who the father of her baby really was? That summer, Miles died of a sudden heart-attack in Golden Square and Angie was distraught.'

Hot tears tracked down my face. My eyes blurred and I wiped them away, angry with myself, with life. 'And Angie?' I said.

Diane described a cold wintery Soho night, with neon lights flashing from the Raymond Revue Bar. She found Angie in the adjacent alley that was full of garbage, piled up, teetering, waiting to be taken away by the bin men. She'd been beaten within an inch of her life and died later that night. They saved the baby but not her.

The baby. Me.

Persuasion

We were in the field, the one all the teenagers went to when trying out smoking, drinking, and the Big Thing. I was just sixteen, Kurt a few months younger.

His best friend, Jonathon Black, was always with us and I was often glad of his company. I preferred Jonathon to Kurt but didn't think anything about that at the time. Jonathon was more my type; bookish and clever, and he was funny, too. Why he wanted to hang about with us, I didn't know. I guessed Kurt had some sort of hold over him, like he did over me. Kurt was charming, amusing, and funny in a put down sort of way, and everyone loved him. Those on the outside were taken in by his boyish charm, with the charisma of this jolly chubby kid. Kurt had a way, an appeal, a cheek, but for some reason, he needed either one of us, or both, with him at all times. I guess he needed an entourage. When either of us wasn't there, he played one off against the other, trying to make the absent one jealous. Everywhere he went, we had to follow. I didn't know what was wrong in Jonathon's life, but I was insecure, under confident, and easy to manipulate. Thirty-five years later, I'm not that person, and I hope, neither is Jonathon but back then, it was all so different.

It was a fresh sunny evening at the end of April. We went walking, the three of us, and ended up in Hobson's fields sitting beneath a thick old tree, fragrant in blossom. I picked petals off daisies, worrying about our pending 'O' levels. The boys talked of transit vans and how they wished they could drive. The early evening sun was delicious, and I warmed my back against it. Large solid cows stood in the adjacent field, flicking their tails, and eyelashes, adding an occasional low lazy 'moooo'. Horses neighed and snuggled together. Gurgling little dove noises were soft in the trees above us. There was nobody around, only us three, and the rich smell of spring that was peaceful and offered false security.

Without warning, Kurt sent Jonathon off and told him to sit down the bank, over the other side of the field. Jonathon hesitated. I sensed he didn't want to go when he stood and looked at me, faltering. I didn't know what

Kurt was up to. I looked at Jonathon and shrugged so he left. I watched him stepping down the bank towards the stream and I knew he'd throw pebbles, trying to skim them. He was the best at skimming stones across the stream.

Once we were alone Kurt pushed me back, flat against the rough grass. The hard ground was lumpy and pressed into my shoulders. He lobbed himself on top of me and I was squashed by this big hefty boy who started slobbering over my face. He wasn't ever the passionate type and he started acting up, moaning, groaning, and told me I was supposed to enjoy it.

I laughed, thinking he was joking. I tried to lift his shoulders off me.

Kurt glared. 'Take your pants off.'

I protested, tugging my short skirt down, trying to tuck it between my legs as I lay beneath him.

'It's time,' he said, quiet, menacing, his hot breath in my face.

'No, it's not!' I started to struggle. I panicked and felt my face flush.

He spat a whisper in my ear. 'Yes. It is.'

'But Jonathon—'

'He's not looking.' Kurt pushed his weight into me.

'No! It's not right. It doesn't feel right,' I protested, trying to my move my slim body from beneath him. I was becoming numb, trapped.

'Oh yes, it's right all right,' he said as he stared at me with steel in his cold blue eyes, his chest pressing on top of me.

Tears prickled my eyes and I struggled to see, tried to blink them away as I tried not show weakness. He hated girls crying though he'd made me upset enough times to see it happen often enough. The rich sickening manure of the field animals reached me as I lay on the ground. Nausea knotted in my tummy and I swallowed the bile that I coughed up in my struggle.

With power in his fists and menace in his eyes, Kurt said, 'Do it.'

So, I did. He leant to one side as he opened his zip. I saw a flash of lemon-yellow underpants and tried not to look. I felt his repellent snake-like skin push against me on my bare thigh as he tried to force his way up my skirt.

'I don't feel anything,' he said, as he tried to force his soft self into me.

155

He grunted, went bright red in the face, and then pushed hard, sharp, like a blade. I gasped. It hurt, really hurt. Kurt didn't move for longer than a few seconds, his weight pressing on me.

I struggled to breathe and kept catching my breath in the back of my throat which was sore with the sour bile.

He moved forward and pushed his weight into me again and stayed there for a moment, breathing heavily into my neck, jelly jowls hanging hot against my cheek. He stabbed himself into me once more, rested, then again, and again, and it hurt with a searing hot pain.

A tear slid down the side of face, running a path down my temple into my hairline. I closed my eyes tight. Everything was bright scarlet beneath my eyelids. I didn't want to see him, see his face as he hurt me again and again. Then he grunted for the last time and it was over.

'You're rubbish!' he said, as he jumped up, cherry-red in the face. He zipped himself up, laughing, and yelled, 'Jonathon!'

He turned me and said, 'Sort yourself out, your clothing is all creased. Is that a strapless bra your wearing? Slut! You better not be pregnant. I don't want a child bride. You'll have to get rid of it if you are.'

I tried to tidy myself up while Kurt whistled and goaded the birds in the trees by throwing clods of earth up at them.

Jonathon arrived back a minute later, and Kurt said, 'It's done.'

Jonathon couldn't meet my eye and I needed him to. He would understand. We were both victims of this cruel person, this boy not yet a man. We both suffered his punches, his taunts, and his lifestyle, and weak that we were, we both stayed, trapped and silent. And we both knew.

That was my first time. Kurt called it persuasion. I called it bullying.

Now I know. It's something completely different.

Remembrance

The gentle strains of *Ave Maria* echoed around the high vaulted chapel of the crematorium. In the back room, Joe was raking the remnants of the first cremation of the day into the hopper, ready for cooling. The digital thermometer on the wall mocked the workers' discomfort with a red flash as it flicked up another notch, showing eighty-two degrees as the clock beneath displayed *11:15:15*. The next service would be over soon, the third that morning. Preparing the cremator for the next body, Joe wiped his brow with the crook of his arm. *Changes*, he mused. Like the new issue polo-shirts instead of overalls, like the new health and safety regulations, like the staff, like life, but not at all like death. The biggest change would always remain the same.

Joe turned to his colleague and said, 'I take my holiday in August, did HR tell you?'

'They mentioned something…what the hell's the heat like then?' Marty asked, blowing out his cheeks. Marty, an ex-social worker, was four weeks into a twelve-week course studying for the BTEC Diploma in Cremation Operations. The certificate required one hundred cremations, completion of which was time reliant upon the death rate of the small city and outlying districts. Seasonal fluctuations meant that eight cremations a day was not unusual during the winter months but in the summer, eight a day, although a rarity, was hot, hard work.

Joe chuckled. 'Why do you think I take it off? You've got a couple of months to learn the ropes before then. Besides, it's quieter in summer. You're learning fast, Marty. From start to finish, body to ashes, ashes to container, how long?'

'Roughly ninety minutes for cremation, cooling an hour, then cremulating. That takes ten to fifteen minutes, depending on the size of the body, give or take a few feet and inches, pounds and ounces…three to four hours in total.'

Joe nodded his agreement.

Marty moved across to the wall-mounted CCTV screens. He watched, arms folded, waiting for the current service to end. 'When there's two cremators going at once...and it's three o'clock on a hot day...I'll feel like I'm in the cremator myself.'

'You get used to it,' mumbled Joe, peering through the sight glass into the dull, red haze checking for any last bits he might have missed in the raking.

'What do you make of that mate?' asked Marty, pointing to the screen showing the chapel. 'No guests, just the Rev reading the 'Lord is My Shepherd' in the chapel with the coffin.'

'Sounds like a game of Cluedo to me, mate.' Laughed Joe.

'No friends, no relatives...just a good quality coffin and a single red rose. Who would do that?'

'Dunno. What's the name?' Joe asked, labelling the container under the cooling tray with the name of the remains he'd just cremated. *Johnson Henry Brownlee.* Sounds like the name of a soul singer, he mused, wondering if the guy had been black.

'Er...' Marty ruffled his papers. 'Maria Rose Capelli, date of birth...would make her...eighty-seven. Do you know her?'

'Rose Capelli? And it's did, not do, we're dealing with the dead, remember,' Joe looked at Marty over the top of his glasses. 'Hmm…Rose Capelli…interesting woman…no wonder there's no congregation.'

'What d'you mean?' Marty asked, as watched on the screen as the plush curtains closed once the Reverend had finished speaking. He prepared to open the double doors for the coffin to come along.

'Well connected. Well…she was, years ago. Didn't know her personally of course. Here, do you want a hand with that?' Joe walked over to Marty and nodded at the casket. 'Lots of history here mate.'

'Oh yeah? Go on then.'

Joe heard the interest spike in Marty's voice. He was going to enjoy this. 'Let's get her loaded first.'

They worked together in the increasing heat, lifted the coffin onto the rollers, ready to charge the cremator with Maria Rose Capelli and her single deep-red fragrant rose.

'Last one until two o'clock,' said Marty. As he closed the door on Rose, he checked the computer screen showed the right settings. The main burner ignited above the coffin. He stood back to watch the process in action, to ensure there were no problems in the important first twenty minutes.

Joe warmed to his theme. 'Rosie here, she could've been famous, made her name. Had she wanted to.'

'Why? What did she do?'

'Not what she did…more like who she was. American, by birth. What do you know about the Prohibition Era?'

'Not a lot, gangster warfare, illegal drinking clubs, that sort of thing. Bugsy Malone is about it. Saw it at the pictures as a kid.'

'Rosie came to England after the war…1947 or thereabouts.' Joe looked at the card Marty had slotted into place to show the name and details of the body inside the cremator. 'Yeah, look, 1922. She'd have been twenty-five then. Came to seek her good fortune…and a man. Got both…for a while.'

Marty nodded encouraging Joe to continue.

'Of course, Capelli's not her real name,' said Joe, building up to full throttle. 'Her mother, May O'Malley, beautiful Irish woman, they adopted it when they went into hiding in Arkansas. Hot Springs. When the chance to move overseas came, well, they took it…got herself a nice little nest egg…services rendered and what not. Child maintenance they'd call it these days.'

'How do you know this?' asked Marty.

'Heard it from my Nan, a bit of folklore history, third generation English-Italian. I get Joe after my granddad, Giuseppe. Anyways, when they came to London, May got on with a barrister type. She was used to gents, but not the English kind…and she had too many edges that needed rounding and a few too many secrets. When the syphilis wormed its way into her brain, she sometimes forgot who she was and talked like who she'd been.'

Marty spluttered, laughing, 'Syphilis? Come on!'

'You might laugh, our Maria…or rather Rosie…poor lass was born with it. Her half-brother, he nearly went deaf…but his dad took him to the best doctors. Those born out of wedlock, like Rosie, poor bastards, they didn't get the same treatment.' Joe pointed into the cremator through the sight glass. 'That coffin's burning pretty quick, Marty, keep an eye on the readings.'

Marty checked the computer screen, watching for changes.

Joe said in a whisper, 'You got that flask, lad?'

'It's in my locker.' Marty bent his head to reply in a whisper, 'But I can go get it if you fancy?'

'Well, shouldn't really, but it's so damn hot in here. A wee sip of tea'll quench the thirst.'

Once Marty had gone, Joe mulled over the tale he was about to tell.

Marty returned a couple of minutes later and handed Joe a cup.

'Best put that flask in the cupboard, just in case of unexpected visitors. You know what these health and safety regs are like. Don't want to get caught drinking on the job, even if it is only tea.' Joe chuckled. 'Something hot in a crematorium? We might burn ourselves. Ha!' He chuckled again. 'So…May died in 1950. Shame. Rosie was a looker but a whore's girl and a gangster for a father…' Joe tut-tutted. 'What was she supposed to do?'

'A whore and a gangster? Yeah, okay. All families have skeletons and secrets and fantasies and lies.' Grinned Marty.

'You know who her father was? Ach, you won't believe me, anyway.' Joe took a slurp of tea and continued, 'Her mother was a great gal. Was a favourite of the sheriff and the judge and the gangster. They always asked for

May. After all, when Mr Big comes to play, the best girls were always available. Yeah, best little whorehouse in Chicago, the Four Deuces down on South Wabash.'

'Think I've heard of that. Or was that the one in Texas?'

'Don't be daft, lad, that was a film with Dolly Parton…Best Little Whorehouse in Texas.' Joe tutted, raising his eyebrows.

'And Burt Reynolds. I remember it now. So…who was Mr Big?'

Joe finished off his dregs and peered into the small round glass window, checking on Rosie. 'Once May gave birth to his daughter, she became his kept mistress. Sent her off to one of his hideaways after she'd had the bairn. With a wife and a son, he didn't want to upset the status quo, did he? May was happy enough, apart from a dose of the syph. She was out of that bordello and changed her name, all that a whore could dream of.'

'*Pretty Woman*,' mused Marty.

'Julia Roberts, Richard Gere.'

'Good film. My eldest loves it but I told her, don't be getting any ideas. She's only thirteen. Kids, eh?'

'Aye, kids. Well this one, Rosie, with her history, an Italian name not only sounded good, but looked it too. That's where the Maria came from.' He took another look through to the cremulator. 'Think there's about forty minutes left, Marty. See that there?' Joe indicated a perfect sphere glowing rose red. 'That's a hip replacement…they don't burn, just discolour. We put 'em in the metal bin and they all get buried in the grounds…'less the family want it, but they never do.'

'Wonder why nobody came?' said Marty. 'I guess you being a cop all those years, you learnt all this stuff?'

'Ten years in the crem taught me well too, but being ex-old bill has its own rewards. Not least the pension.' He tipped a wink. 'Rosie grew up a lovely girl. Big daddy doted on her, but she didn't see much of him…and nothing once he moved to Florida. He always sent her mother a red rose on Valentine's Day though, Rosie's birthday.'

'Ahh. Right. The red rose,' Marty nodded.

'I suppose it was what she wanted, just one rose. Significant. The memory…something like that.'

'So, what did she do once her mother died?'

'The same Harrington-Smythe that her mother took up with then took up with her. Her silky, black Irish hair and bright sparky eyes, she was a right doppelganger for a younger May.'

'Like mother like daughter eh?' Marty winked back.

'She was nothing like her mother. She was no whore. Far from it. She'd been sheltered from a lot of that life. Oh, she knew the gangsters…Jonny Torrio, Big Jimmy Cosimo, and all their mob. She knew about the bootlegging, the cards, the ladies…but don't forget, she'd been taken out of that seedy side of life. She was protected.'

'Confusing for a kid…exciting though,' said Marty, watching the body reduce to ashes.

'Yeah. She put it to good use thought, her knowledge. With the help of her rich sugar daddy, she set up hostels for prostitutes, like safe houses for the street walkers. She hated to see them beaten, battered, broken, knew what the pimps were like, had heard the stories from her mother and the aunties back in the states. She knew how privileged she'd been to escape. It could have been the same for her…'

'Like social work then.'

'Something like that…she set up in East London to start with. Was offered the OBE you know…but turned it down. She was happy getting on with her missions, rescuing the poor lost souls, arranging black market abortions, talking to the women who'd been raped, beaten, those who'd lost who they were. They'd call it counselling today.'

'Sad.'

'Yeah, but positive. Another Marie Stopes in a way, but from the other side of life. Same philosophies though.'

'Vera Drake.'

'Her an' all.'

'Wonder why she wasn't she called Maria? It's such a pretty name.'

'Good question Marty. Her father would have liked Rose, after his sister who'd died as a baby, but his daughter was illegitimate, born to a whore. As a first name it seemed disrespectful, so she was given Maria…it just never got used.'

'Go on then, who was her old man?'

'She was nothing like her old man either. Not a bad streak in her.'

'He was a bad 'un, then?'

'Have a guess?' Marty laughed.

'I have no idea, mate.'

'He was the Big One, Big Al. Scarface himself.'

'What! No…not Al Capone?' Marty took a step back, glanced into the cremator and back at Joe. 'Never!'

'Oh yes, the very one. It's not logged in any official document of course. He had illegitimate kids all over the states. Women seem to like the bad boys.' Joe smiled.

'Can't believe it.'

'She kept it to herself, pretty much.'

'But why no friends? To see her off?'

'She never wanted any fuss. Didn't want it known, the fame, the celebrity…just wanted a quiet life, doing her own thing. Bless her. Imagine her on the Jerry Springer show? Or Jeremy Kyle? And anyway, she'd never had family of her own.'

'Well, Joe. You just never know, do you?' said Marty, fluctuating between open-mouthed wordlessness and shaking his head.

'You never do. I always think it's such a shame. Fractions of time pass by and we don't notice, like the wind that disappears on a calm day, or a familiar presence we miss in an over-crowded room. We don't see them at all, and we wish we had. We'll never know what these people are, who they really were, and now it's all too late. The only thing we can do is remember them in our own individual way.'

'How poetic.' Marty looked quite sad.

'Blimey, I'm witnessing an epiphany,' said Joe, hiding a smile. 'Comes with the job mate.'

'Well, you just changed my day, mate.'

'Thank you. I think she's got half an hour left. You rake out this time, you need the practice. I'll take Mr Johnson Brownlee, the soul singer, down to the cremulator. Won't be long.'

JOE LOOKED INTO the container and saw a small knobble and idly wondered whether if it was part of something or a whole something. He fitted the large funnel attachment and emptied the contents into the cremulator. The metal and granite balls clattered around in the machine, grinding the remains into ashes. Retirement was looking good. As long as the research and the basics were right, he might even be able to make a third career from writing short stories from his cremated characters. He'd always loved inventing lives for them. Maria was one of his best yet.

Joe, who was English without any hint of Italian, smiled as he mused on Mr Johnson Brownlee. Perhaps he could make him the first openly gay black soul singer?

Haemorrhage

He moves from the kitchen to the diner, flat-footed and fat, scratching himself through his washed-out saggy boxers. He lifts his fingers to his face, sniffs, then turns to me and sneers. I'm compelled to watch this ritual. He disgusts me as much as I know I must disgust him. His belch is echoed by a rippling fart as he exhales, looking at me a crooked smile. I dry-cry silent tears, forced to sit in the foggy stench and observe the despicable creature that is my husband.

He sets about frying himself a crispy egg. I could have told him the fat was too hot, that's why he burns the edges. In another world I'd have been doing it for him so there wouldn't be any need to say anything, but this is far from that parallel universe.

He spreads butter across two slices of thick toastie bread, pours ketchup which oozes from the crusts like drops of thick blood. Mesmerised, I fantasise that the blood is mine. If only. A pint pot of tea steams in a stained mug that he never cleans properly. Milk. He needs milk, but he left it out last night and now it's curdled. He curses and rips the top off a new carton, spilling the first few drops into the frying pan and it sizzles. The sight would be worthy of a comedy sketch in that other world if it wasn't so desperate and sad.

Lisa is coming today so I know he'll make a paltry effort to tidy up. He knows she'll do it, clean up after him, our daughter with her five kids by three fathers. I sit and cry my silent tears. There is little else I can do.

'HI, MAM!' LISA drops her bulging bags to the floor, and she's followed into the house by three children. 'Where's Dad? Upstairs I suppose. How are you today? Stop that, Ryan! Get your hands out of the cat-tray.'

She yanks her three-year-old by his coat collar and he fights back, punching her in the crotch. I don't wonder where he saw that. Her latest beau is as bad as the others before him but at least he gives her money, a first for solvency in her house.

Lisa sits the children in the front room and puts a kiddie channel on the television. 'Now stay put!' she shouts at them and closes the door. 'Want some dinner, Mam?'

Three hours later, she has fed and dressed me, washed my hands and face, and brushed my hair. She's a good kid, doesn't deserve this life. But then, which one of us does?

Lisa, pregnant at fifteen, hell, what rows we had, me and her. She never said who Donny's father was, but when it was years too late, I guessed. By then I was unable to do or say anything. When Lisa comes to visit, I see it in her eyes, and her son's, and her father's. They each have the same face. She can't bear to look me in the eye, and I know how she feels. If I was her, I wouldn't be able to look at me either. I've let her down.

I've had a lot of time to think in the last three years. Perhaps this is my penance. Confined to this awful cumbersome chair, unable to talk, walk, live a life. I long for the day of the black light, the dark blinding pain and numbness gone. I wish it would come for me and when it does, for it surely will, I don't want any sort of recovery. The doctors expected it to come soon after the stroke, but I sit and wait and pray it comes quick.

Lisa wipes my saliva and talks nonsense to me. They think I don't understand what they say but oh, how I do, spoken and unspoken. I look at my daughter, ragged with nerves, dulled with an ugly beauty, too much life for a girl of her age.

I remember when she was born, just me and her in the house, her father on a three-day bender. I loved her, love her, very much, but it all went wrong in the bitter lemon of life. I know I should have left but where could I have gone? I had no one but Lisa, and I thought staying was the right thing to do, for her, if not for me. He used to love us, I'm sure of it, until he started beating me. By then it was too late. I was stuck. I'd only wanted to give her the chances and security I never had. I could have been a somebody, once. I had a working brain, a life, a future. Then my mum died, and I was alone, scared, and abused. When I met him, I thought we could have a life.

I want to reach out my hand and touch Lisa's blonde hair, as if the feel of my fingers will turn it from bland wiry straw into the glossy princess she once was. I see her standing there, with her bosom sagging down to her stomach-rolls, and stomach-rolls hanging down to her pelvis, and I remember her as a slim, dancing girl dressed up as a Turkish belly-dancer. How we laughed when we saw how good she was at it.

'Mam, look! I can do it!' She sounded as surprised as we were.

I hugged her tight, kissed her forehead, and loved her more, my beautiful twelve-year-old daughter. That's when his real interest sparked. I worked it out, sitting in this chair when I had nothing else to do but think about the years gone by. I should have noticed – the way she covered herself up, even in the summer, the self-harm marks on her inner-arm, the dour look on her face when I had to go to work and leave her with him. I blamed her attitude on her and I blamed her for being a teenager. And then she was pregnant.

I THOUGHT MY heart had broken the day Lisa left me to live on the eighth floor of Hansard House. She took her baby boy, a suitcase of clothes and the fifty quid I'd saved for her.

'I need my own place now Mam. I know you'll be all right. And I'll visit all the time.' She smiled at me, gave me a tight hug, and was gone.

I never stopped worrying. The no-good wasters she took home because they were looking for love. Then they'd leave her with a black eye, a bust face, an empty purse, a trashed house, a dose of the clap, or belly full of arms and legs.

It didn't have to be this way and now it is. We're a family stuck on repeat like an old 45 single. I then realised I knew nothing about broken hearts when Lisa left. That was a pain yet to come.

THE KIDS START fighting in the front room and I hear something smash. I cringe as Lisa shouts out, 'Ryan! You little bastard! What have you done to Chelsea?'

The stinging slap sounds like hurt and I grit my worn-down teeth.

I wish she wouldn't bring them, not because I don't love them, but I know it's boring for them here. And I'm not a pretty sight. They only come with her because she can't get a minder. She looks after me and their granddad is either pissed, out in the bookies, or vile and angry. They sit and play, make a mess, and fight. I long to pick them up, take them to play in the park, treat them like the little babies he stopped me from having myself and it truly breaks my heart when the little ones ask in their innocent way, '*Why is nanny like that?*' '*Why doesn't she speak, or walk, or feed herself like normal nannies?*' '*Why doesn't she give us pocket money like Jack's nana?*'

Lisa finishes tidying my house but leaves the washing-up. She goes home with the kids and that's the last I'll see of her until Monday. 'Take care of yourself, Mam, don't let him bully you,' she says every time she leaves. As if I have a choice and as if she doesn't know.

If only they'd put me in Grasmere Lodge. It's the damn carer's allowance that did it. When he found out how much he'd get for looking after me at home he knew he could be as lazy as he liked. He soon packed in looking for work, not that he ever had much in the way of work. It also meant he could get bladdered every night without a nagging, not that I was ever able to stop him drinking, and not that he ever did much caring. He did sort out a catheter for me but for his benefit, not mine.

Whenever he could bring himself to change them, the huge, rancid nappies were flung and piled up in the corner of my room. My room, the one the council paid someone to come and convert for me when we moved into the special bungalow. My room is also the one he uses for his scrap-metal junk. Of course, I'm not a kid, and nobody comes to check up on me, the social have done their bit, don't care as I'm not a priority. I'm being looked after. They think. When the worst infection set in, the nurse could tell he'd left me in the same nappy for some days and nights. A catheter was best for everyone, she said, if he wasn't coping. He got the sympathy then, and I got thrush and antibiotics. It doesn't make much difference to me, it's all part of my existence. Now when the piss overflows the bag, it's a bit of swearing and a slapping about the head until he's had enough of the sport that is Connie-bashing.

He did have a woman, for a while. She didn't last long; only as long as he could sustain the charm, which was never more than a few weeks. The upstairs bedroom hadn't seen so much activity. She was sort of nice, I suppose. At least she talked to me and fed me breakfast, something I never get from him. She made me up, once, with pink lipstick and thick mascara. It felt good. He gave her slap and kick up the backside as she walked out of the door. I never saw her again and he stopped bringing his women round so much after that. I think at first, he thought one of them would take over looking after me if they moved in with him, become my carer, but then I think he realised they might report him to the social or something. I heard a voice threaten it once and never heard her again. That was another one who never came back, or maybe it was in my head and wishful thinking, dreaming.

LISA FORGOT TO put me by the window. I'll sit here, staring at a crusted cooker oozing stale sticky fat until he bothers to turn me around. I suppose he told her not to put me by the front again. The last time he found me looking outside, he shouted, 'Who wants to see your fucking ugly mug staring at them as they walk past? You're enough to frighten the neighbourhood dogs, you fucking mong.' I suppose he had a point.

He kicked my wheels around and hoisted the chair in the corner, not bothering or caring that I was looking at the full sink. The weeks' worth of washing-up is piled up because Lisa rebelled and refused to do it. I remember how tidy I had to keep the home or risk a beating. Thankfully, I passed that down to Lisa and she's very house-proud, the only control she has in her own hard life.

I think about tomorrow. Tomorrow's Friday. Fridays are poker nights. Poke-er Nights, as he calls them. I hate Fridays. They're the worst. His pub-scum mates come around looking for something a bit more. Despicable men, they're sort of hooked on it now and as much as it might have disgusted them in the beginning, a few stuck around and the evillest ones come back for more.

All I want to do is die. Anything would be better than this. I'd rather be in a home, smelling of wee and eating mushed-up peas and carrots than be used by him and his grotesque gang of gargoyles. I close my eyes and beg inside please put me out of misery and I dream of a pillow over my face and look for the black light which doesn't come. You can eat all you want when I am properly dead for I am dead inside already, only a sick heartbeat keeping me alive.

AND NOW IT'S Friday and time for my weekly wash and brush up. He cleans me up good and proper and makes me smell nice with fresh clean clothes. Sometimes he pays Angela down the road to bed-bath me and do my hair, put on a bit of make-up, spray a blast of perfume. She thinks she's doing it for him, and I watch them flirt and I know she's giving him the sympathy shag because his pathetic stroke-wrenched wife can't. It's in the eyes. I've become good at reading eyes.

Then it's time. It's seven o'clock. And the men come.

Baby Butterfly

I stitch wings on the back of my baby's dress. I do it every day. I do it so she can fly. One day she will need them and then she won't need me anymore.

I HAD A different baby, once. A baby boy, all dressed in blue, with crinkles in his tiny face, and smells of damp frogs and snails and full of puppy dog tails, like a boy should be. He had a dimple in his left cheek but not his right. A black tick licked his head with hair, and I called him Tom, like Tom Thumb.

They took him away.

But I always had my thumb. Whenever I thought of him I'd take my thumb into my mouth, fill it up with Tom, and suck, hard, like he wanted to suckle me when he was a newborn baby, but they wouldn't let him because they said it wasn't the done thing.

They came and took him away on the fifth day. I was fifteen and six months. They said it was the right thing to do, those people from social services, those from St David's Vicarage, and my parents, and the people who wanted him for their own. They took my baby away.

Dad didn't speak to me ever again, but I didn't mind that. He only ever spoke to me to tell me off, or dictate teenage terms, like what time I had to be home, and what time I had to get out of bed, and what company I could keep. Like that could stop me doing things he didn't want me to do.

Then they took my baby boy, Tom, and I didn't care if I never spoke to my father at all.

'You have to understand, Marisa. He's your father. He has standards.' My mother tried hard to explain, tried hard to defend him, and I saw the look in her eye. She was frightened of him.

I didn't get it. I sucked hard on my thumb. 'Why didn't he never love me?' I asked.

She couldn't answer. She pushed her hands deep into the pocket of her housewife's pinny and she scuffed the black slate floor with her worn slippers. She looked sad with her down-turned mouth and shuttered eyes and wrinkles that belonged to a woman of older years.

'I love you, Marisa,' was all she said.

I knew she meant it.

I WAS CARELESS. I lost her. I lost my baby. I did everything I could to keep her with me but sometimes, no matter what, they go away anyway. And now I can't find her. I can't see her cherub face with sweet pudgy squeaky cheeks, and plump rosebud lips, and big big eyes that look at me with the love and trust of a baby to its mama. I can't smell her, all sugar and spice and all things nice. I don't know where to find her. I think they may have taken her like they took Tom. The tears prickle behind my eyes like they belong to somebody else. I can't see no more. I scrabble about the bed, pat-pat the blankets, and move the floor. I look under the bed, in the cupboard in the corner, in the bottom drawer of the plastic topped unit. I laugh. Maybe she is locked in the lavatory? But I know she isn't.

Then it's panic over. I let her down. Gently. I let her fall like a feather, taken by the wind, so she could float. I wanted to see if she could fly.

They said she didn't feel the pain. But how do they know? Did they ask her? Could she say? I didn't know babies could talk. What makes them think they understand?

I needed to see if she could fly and who, when I'm not there for her, would catch her?

I slump back onto the bed in the corner of the room that's full of beds just like mine. The beds are full of bodies that belong to people I don't know and don't like. The smell of polish tries to disguise the smell of bleach and other disinfectants that the women in pink coats use to hide the smells of the people and the things they've done. Things that I think might be bad. Things I don't want to know about.

I suck Tom Thumb and think of him, my son, and I think of her, my daughter, Candy, who smelt so nice. They are my babies. I had to let them go.

I STITCH WINGS on the back of my baby's dress. I do that every day. I do it every day so she can fly. One day, like today, when I'm not with her, she will need them, and she won't need me anymore. She'll flutter away to freedom. My baby butterfly.

Red Herrings

It was one hundred steps from the ferry side to the clubhouse. It was one hundred steps to be out of range of the best CCTV that today's money could buy. One hundred steps, fifty double strides, about one hundred yards, perhaps ninety metres, more or less, depending on height, size of feet, age, and intent of the stepper. It can be walked in less than two minutes, or ran in about ten seconds, if ultra-fast. Fifteen by some, longer by many. It was one hundred steps too many for Sue-Mo Ray.

DI Angela Panter picked up the pack of SOCO photographs that had landed on her desk, typically late with a curt apology and the usual excuses. She flipped the front cover to reveal the crooked body of Sue-Mo Ray as it lay on the cracked paving slabs of Red Square on the

Moscow Estate, the most notorious patch of criminality in their whole district.

It had been snowing and the frosted covering gave the impression of sugary sweetness, cosy warm houses, and pristine pathways. Angela envisaged delighted children dancing in the sharp air like imps as the flakes floated down, oblivious as the snow started to settle atop the dead body of a local prostitute.

Angela shrugged out of her suit jacket and let it fall onto the office chair as it swivelled behind her. Pages one to four revealed the body from different angles, black and white images stark against the snow. Numbers five, six and seven were scene shots of the surrounding area, on the left, cosy houses belying cosy crime, to the right, a combination of barren and bold corrugated erections for bustling business now long gone apart from the fish house. Photos eight, nine, and ten concentrated on the body again, the head from neck upwards, wide eyes open, staring at life from the position of death, brown and muddy, the sparkle gone, lips dark and open, like a fish-mouth in the shock of being caught, unable to wriggle away.

Angela picked up the polystyrene container of coffee that one of the team had brought up from the canteen. She peeled the plastic lid, careful not spill the luke-warm liquid as the strong damp bean smell curled up her nose. She took a sip and stared at the photographs, looking, seeing, thinking beyond the obvious, searching to see what lay behind.

It was a red herring. A smoky plot. Something fishy. Detective Inspector Angela Panter was an officer of experience and had canny knowledge with an eye on the bobbing ball. She knew there was more, something she wasn't seeing, and she also knew that pictures often lied.

Like the act of chewing gum, an exercise of mastication, with the flavour long gone, she couldn't spit it out until she knew. The strangulation of a prostitute could possibly be understood. A crime of passion, something a man might do to a woman. She had seen many women who had been murdered, many of them strangled. Strangely, only one man. He'd been strangled by his male partner during an auto-erotic game gone wrong. Strangulation was a crime of force, of power, of will. Of strength. There was nothing accidental about strangling somebody. This crime wasn't that, it was something altogether different. It was a cold kill.

Angela picked up the preliminary pathologist's report, read it, and placed it back onto her desk. She stared at the first photograph again, the full picture, looking but not seeing the body staring back at her. She wondered what the motive really was.

'Carter, what do you think?' she asked, leaning back into the chair as she raised her trousered legs onto the desk, crossing them right over left. Times like this were the times she imagined lighting up and blowing smoke rings into the sour squad room, a hangover from the days when she smoked, when CID offices were full of fug, days before the ban, and a time when she was a trainee, eager for the catch, and not so concerned about her unhealthy habits of smoking, of drinking pints of beer, going for after work curries and sleeping with unsuitable men. God, she blasphemed, reminding herself of a TV cliché. How and when had that happened? Jane Tennison she wasn't. Or maybe she had become?

She asked her cohort again. 'Carter, what do you think?'

Phil Carter ran a finger around his tight collar, bullfrog eyes looking down. 'You know what I think. Same as four hours ago. We've got our man. Don't know why you think it's not him.'

'I never said that. He might have done it. Be as guilty of murder as well as infidelity. But why? Why would he kill her? I don't get it.'

'There isn't always a motive. Could be one of a dozen or more motives. I don't know why you feel you have to get inside their heids. You look too deep.' Carter paused. 'His brief will be here at eight in the morning so who's doing the interview? Mandy Thomas is keen. I can do it with her.'

'Mandy Thomas?' Angela nodded, thinking about the wannabe detective. She mulled it over. Mandy was a girl with ambition, all tits and high cheekbones, but with a clever head on her for someone so young in her career. She was sure Phil Carter would love the chance to do it with her. 'Yes. Perhaps.'

Angela pursed her lips as she wound a few strands of loose dark hair around her fingers like the silky slinky snakes she'd played with as a child. She placed the clutch of hair into her mouth without thinking and chewed down like she'd done forever, ever since sitting on the stairs as a little girl, listening to her parents argue, get drunk, make up, and argue again. She closed her eyes and let her mind drift, letting it do its work. The answer would come, maybe not tonight, but soon.

BERNARD FLETCHER, MD of North Sea Herring International languished in the cells overnight. In the morning, his eyes were sore and his manner one of bewilderment and some distress. Phil Carter thought it was an act. Angela Panter wasn't so sure.

Did Bernard Fletcher love her, this woman they'd picked up from the back of the workingman's drinking club, discarded by the rubbish bins, cold dead, just one hundred steps from his fish depot? Not a chance. But did he like her? Angela Panter guessed so. His tears for Sue-Mo seemed real, looked real, genuine concern for the woman who he paid to do the things his wife wouldn't. His questions weren't about what would happen to him. He didn't protest his innocence as one might expect. He wasn't demanding in any way for a man accused of murder. He was concerned about his wife and how she was coping. He was concerned for the little girl from the nearby estate who had found the dead body while waiting outside for her dad to come out of the clubhouse. How would it affect her? Would she forever have nightmares, he asked? He apologised for his dishevelled appearance, stating he hadn't had a good night and said he knew he needed a shower as he could smell his body odour and taste his rancid breath.

It might be a brilliant act by their prime suspect, worthy of an equity card, but Angela Panter didn't think so. She thought about the profile of the kind of man who may do this kind of thing. The profile of someone who would kill a prostitute and dump her body one hundred yards or so from his own workplace.

A man like Bernard Fletcher, a man who had money, status, and power, would have a lady at home waiting for him, manicured and picture-perfect with her painted nails and painted lips that hid expensive dentist-white teeth but never revealed passionate smiles. This other lady, the one on the slab, the one who led a life of debauchery, drugs, and ultimate destruction, might have blackened-by-life teeth, but she laughed. Oh, how she laughed. And smiled. And gave him fun. It was the fun he paid for, not the sex. A man like Bernard Fletcher wanted someone to laugh at his silly jokes, someone who let him treat her the way he wanted to treat her, and it didn't include the best material goods. He wanted someone to smile back at him when he smiled at her. The woman on the slab was someone who would let him run his smoky-stubby fingers down her cheek without fear of soiling three-layered foundation and pink-puff powder that cost him large on his credit card.

Maybe a male detective would let the little clues pass him by. Perhaps he didn't, wouldn't, couldn't see it – the red herring. Perhaps he wouldn't take the bait. Perhaps someone like detective sergeant Phil Carter, a man Angela knew wanted her rank and wanted her job, would be blind to the evidence. But for the female 'tec, for DI Angela Panter, the case wormed away like a struggling fish on the end of a line, tempting, waiting to be caught.

As she suspected, Bernard Fletcher denied murder when questioned by DS Carter and acting DC Thomas. He exercised his right to a solicitor and chose to answer all questions. DI Panter watched from the observation room adjacent to the tiny interview cell. Fletcher spoke with his workingman's hands, cried with his heart, and admitted to liking the company of prostitutes, especially Sue-Mo, his favourite, but he refuted all allegations against him with emotion and passion and the non-verbal cues of an innocent man.

Angela Panter chewed on her long dark strands as she watched the interview unravel. Fletcher had been to the club for a meet with two men who owed him, two guys who worked in the packing section of his warehouse. They had been doing a bit of dodgy business for him on the side, a bit of tax evasion to the sum of a quarter of a million pounds. Small fry in the whole operation but enough to worry Fletcher when the police interviewed him. But did avoiding duties to the Inland Revenue make him a murderer?

He was in the right place. At the right time. Or the wrong time, for him. And then she had it. The answer was there all the time. A man might strangle to murder but this body, this locally known prostitute who had a penchant for rich men, hadn't been strangled. There was no sex-before-death either. There was no struggle. No sloppy evidence to mop up. This had been a clean kill.

DI Panter knew her suspect.

A man might shoot and leave but only a woman would shoot to kill.

DI Angela Panter allowed herself a satisfied smile when she sent the troops to arrest the suspect. Angela Panter had her catch and she wasn't about to let her wriggle away.

It was only one hundred steps. It can be walked in less than two minutes, or ran in about ten seconds, if ultra-fast. Fifteen by some, longer by many. It was only one hundred steps from the ferry side to the clubhouse. It was one hundred steps too many for Mrs Margaret Fletcher, wife to the MD of North Sea Herring International.

The Same Face

His hand hovered above the pristine bed sheet. A knotted ball of worms twisted and turned in his gut as the nightmare memories bubbled. A shiver of fear ran down his back and trickled cold sweat down between his buttocks as the past became the present and he looked into that face. Her face. He would never forget that face.

Her calloused hand touched his skin like it had been yesterday that she'd grabbed him upwards with a vicious yank, dragging him to his bare and blistered feet. The same brutal hand that today lay withered and wrinkled atop the crisp hospital bed, fresh just for her, the new patient on the ward.

He looked at the fingers, clawed, gnarled and hard with nails that looked too large for the arthritic hand that belied the deeds it had dealt. Both wicked and innocent at the same time. How could such a hand inflict torture?

And why should old age become an excuse for sins of the past?

He brought his eyes up to look at her. At that face. The features were the same; the slight hook-nose with the sneering pinch of disgust, the half-open blue eyes that were sharp and cold, thin lips parted slightly to allow shallow breaths to escape. The shallow breaths replaced the sharp words she'd spat at him when he was a boy. Her sunken cheeks did nothing to soften the image and today she was old. Aged. And within him, there was no forgiveness.

He couldn't stop the memories. *Flash. Flash. Flash.* He was drowning, felt his heartbeat quicken, the drum-drumming hard inside his chest, and it hurt. The pound-pounding in his right temple made him light-headed, dizzy and nauseous, so he steadied himself by her bed as he stood at ease, an old habit she'd enforced and one he'd never forgotten. As he stood there, remembering, he felt the warm wet groin of his trousers and was transported back to that thin scabby boy of eight who lived in foster-care with an older couple, a nice, steady, reliable family. They already had two foster boys, so it seemed perfect for a poor orphan child, like Mark. They made sure all the boys were subject to the same treatment. And the boys learnt to be grateful.

Mark developed an unsociable habit. When Mother beat them, he would wet the bed. The more he wet the bed, the more she'd beat them. One for all and all for one.

Mark stood by her bed and cringed as he remembered the twisted iron poker that cut and bruised his skin. The scars on his back ached with pain and memory, stinging his skin like they were fresh and inflicted yesterday.

'Stand at ease!' she'd bellow until they stood at great unease by the side of the double bed, waiting for the mattress to dry. They stood at unease for hours.

Mark closed his eyes and saw himself, a pathetic animal lying on the soiled mattress, goose-pimpled and trembling as she watched the dancing flame reflect in his eyes. He saw his pupils enlarge, engorged with fear, black, and wide and deep. She held the lit match in her hand, close to his face, so close that he smelt his hair singeing. He sensed her excitement, could smell her exhilaration above her sour perfume. And they both knew he'd do exactly what she told him. Previous inflictions of violence made sure of it. The thrill and power in her eyes made it so. Like a spitting cauldron, her words stung as she spat them out. When she told him to drop his trousers so she could see if he was a man yet, he could do nothing but oblige.

She stepped an inch forward.

He flinched, shrank back, and shivered into the cold corner of his wet bed. She moved closer and laughed again, the special laugh just for him. He was hers, all hers.

SHE REACHED FOR his arm. Held the match to his face. And blew. Smoke curled up into his nostrils, burnt his brain, choked his hope.

She lit another, so close to him he could smell her stale underarm odour. It mingled with sour perfume and scorching matchsticks.

He turned his head to one side.

She lifted his arm and let the little flame dance on the underside of his miniscule bicep.

It tickled. At first. Then burnt. Burnt the scar tissue. He closed his eyes and let his tears fall silent as he tried hard to block out the pain.

IT WAS SUCH a long time ago. Mark had many memories that flickered a reminder at night when he was supposed to be sleeping. In his dreams she'd grown into an ogre-witch of tall-thin proportions, with crooked black teeth, and long straggly hair. She'd become a caricature of all things evil.

He looked at the wizened woman on the bed. If it wasn't for that face, that face he couldn't forget … Mark looked at her. '*How could you?*' '*How could you?*' '*How could you?*'

He placed a bedpan on the table and picked up her chart. Her date of birth showed she was eighty-two. Really? He didn't remember. He read '*intestinal blockage, renal failure, anaemia*'. She was too frail for surgery. He knew she'd be in pain and wouldn't last much longer.

Mark waited until she was conscious, eyes fully open, mind vaguely aware. He'd given her something to liven her up, pep her spirits, to bring her round a bit.

Then he disconnected her catheter.

The geriatric ward was a busy place. Nobody bothered to question why he took on her care, why he was focussed on her needs. Nobody was going to argue or question him. She was one less for anyone else to care about.

He read out her name from the chart. 'Mrs Hargreaves? Edna?'

'Yes, dear,' she whispered. Light. Delicate. Not harsh. Not anymore.

'Hello Edna. Do you remember me?'

'No, dear.' She tried to shake her head. 'Should I?'

'Mark. Mark Campbell, Mrs Hargreaves. I'm Mark.' They never remembered him.

'Mark,' she moved her head, tried to nod. The fine hair he remembered as dark and straggly was now grey and thin. But she had *that* face. The same face. They all had the same face.

'Here's a cup of tea, Edna. And look, a silk headscarf. I remembered how you like them. Shall I lay it across the top of your head, just as you like it?' All the old ladies loved a silk headscarf. She wouldn't be able to resist. He wound the soft material over her head, draping it across her hair.

'Such a lovely boy, a caring boy.' She smiled. 'Thank you.'

He smiled back and tucked in her sheets, despite them not being loose. 'I'll make you comfortable, take away all that pain, all that hurt. I was such a nice boy. Such

202

a quiet boy. Not given to sulking.' He slipped the injection of opium into the frail vein at the crook of her arm. He left the hot sugary tea by her bedside, knowing it would be abandoned, just like he had been.

AN HOUR LATER, the Doctor arrived on the ward to sign the death certificate. 'I hadn't expected her to last the week though I thought she'd have a couple more days. Just her time, I suppose. Any relatives to notify?'

'No. Nobody. The home brought her in yesterday. There are no relatives,' Mark told him.

'Make sure the paperwork's sorted before she's taken off to the mortuary.'

It was. Mark made sure of it. She might not have had much longer left, was dying anyway, but he'd taken control. Taken the power and used it.

He delivered her body to the morgue himself, not lingering for a porter. He whistled as he wheeled her down the corridors, as he stood by her in the lift, and as he pushed her along the halls of the basement. A bubble of ecstasy coursed through him, satiating him at last. For now.

They'd just brought in another. Perhaps she too had been wicked, a tyrant, like the others. Like Edna Hargreaves. Mary Greensides. Violet Murray. Or the first – Nora Scott. Maybe she'd given her husband, or her kids, or someone else's kids, a tortured life. After all, she had the same face. They all had the same face and he saw her everywhere, in every face. Every time they smiled. Every time they looked at him. And he couldn't help himself, couldn't stop himself from what he had to do. He was doing the world a favour, getting rid of all the Edna Hargreaves in the world. She who had made him what he was. He couldn't believe it when he'd first seen her, hiding there, in someone else's body. He'd known it was her, could see it in the face. They all had it.

Saggy Tits and All That

I stood outside in the backyard by the coal bunker trying not to see the black dust and grey grime and moss crawling green up the bricks. I was trying not to think about the outside lav and the odious smells as they curdled up my nose, weaving a path into my sinuses. I had such a heightened sense of smell, it was knocking me sick.

It was then I should have realised. It was always a give-away, a tell-tale sign, but when I saw the blood, relief swept through me. Not this month. Thank the lord. Not this month. And never again, I hoped. If only he'd keep away from me like that. I kept telling him to be careful, but he was having none of it.

TEN DAYS LATER I stood outside again, but this time in the rain, and blowing smoke rings up into the dank air, cold sea-frets coming in from the slippery-rock shore. I watched my cigarette smoke disperse into the air and I

205

had that feeling again, that something wasn't right. I thought about the rumbling tummy, the constant heartburn, the curdling smells, and the waking-up feeling sick. I was short-tempered too, but then I was always short-tempered so maybe the temper wasn't a sign, it was just me. Not that I'd ever admit it the man.

I smoothed down my pinny, fumbled in the front pocket for another match, and lit up the fag again because the rain had put it out. What the feck was I gonna do?

Another kid. An extra mouth on my tit. Just got one off, still had one on, couldn't be doing with another. I felt like one of those factory conveyor belts, one off, one on, one off, one on. I tried hard to think of it as a baby, a growing living thing inside me, another little me. Or another little him. But we already had six of the buggers and eldest only about to turn nine. There was only so much money, so much porridge and forage, only so much I could do with a five time or more hand-me-down. I was knackered and ready for the boards and only thirty-four. Lank hair with no curl, a flabby belly, and tits I could sling under me armpits. I didn't want another bairn. I didn't want no more kids.

I went down to the dispensary in Aviemore Lane once every few days asking for something for the dyspepsia, something for the sickness, something for my foul bad temper and something for my old man to stop me getting in the family way. I took everything they gave me, and more. I took anything I could think of to make it go away, to stop it from growing inside me. To get rid. It was a bit like I was committing a murder but not because it wasn't here yet, alive and kicking, not breathing. Not really anything at all. That's how I made myself think.

Nothing worked, so I tried to think of it as a baby but then I couldn't. It was a thing. Just a growing thing inside me. Like a real live bairn. I couldn't help think of it like one of them yet, with its own face, own features, own personality.

Everywhere I went I had to take the children with me, and I couldn't manage another. I really couldn't. I was never maternal before I had kids, but I did look after them and was a proud mam an' all that. I did me best. It just got me mad these days because I never had a minute to sit down and I was knackered like an auld horse every minute of every day. And I was especially fed up with the tits I could sling under me armpits that weren't attractive anymore and not pert and up and round and sexy like Pat what's-her-name over the way that I saw me old man looking at when he thought I wasn't looking at him.

Every night I wake up and lie sweating with fear about another mouth on the nipple, the red stuck-out berry that wouldn't smooth down like it did when I was sixteen. I'd feel that sucking at me, the draining me dry, and it would be a nightmare and I'd be having those night sweats. I imagined it taking all the life from me and gorging itself on my red-red blood.

I knew I could do nothing else but see the doctor. Get sorted with it and start to prepare. It's time, would be here soon enough, and I would have to tell him, the old man, that there'd be another mouth to feed. Another one of us. Another conglomeration of me and him. And of course, he'd go on the piss for two days and two nights to celebrate another drain on our meagre existence.

When I finally went to see the Doc, my prayers to the lord had been answered. Sort of. There was no baby. No baby. Not this time.

I thought, for one brief minute, the smallest time possible, that it was all okay, and relief flooded through me, up from my toes. I thought for the flicker of a few seconds that it would all be all right.

But it was not all right. It was worse. There was no baby. Never had been a baby. Babbies no more. It wasn't a baby at all but was a definite living thing growing inside me. It was the hugest tumour the doctor had ever known. So he said.

After lots of those horrible tests at the hospital they said there was nothing to be done. It's still growing inside me and after a few months there would be no birth, no mouth on my tit, no combination of me and him a-squealing and a-squawking and I wished I could take it all back to when I stood in the backyard making smoke rings with me fag thinking about names for the baby that never was and wishing it wasn't. I wished it was a baby, saggy tits and all.

This thing I had growing inside would be the death of me.

That Loving Feeling

You don't know what to do. Everything he does irritates. You hate yourself for being so mean, for responding, for being nasty. You can't seem to help it. You try to take it back and smile at him. And he smiles back.

You feel sorry for him. Sympathy makes you make love to him. He thinks that it's all right now and his eagerness makes your guilt rise like bile.

You try to keep it light and the next day you crack open some jokes and smile at him again. Inside, the pounding headache that is your life throbs louder. You have that migraine sickly feeling that makes you want to vomit, and it won't go away with two paracetamols. Neither will he.

You love him, of course you do, but what happened to the spark, the fire in your belly that rose like a backdraft? The flame of passion that filled your head, your heart, and your groin? Where did it go?

You buy him a gift. You tell him you love him. You try to recreate the tingle factor that was once all you lived for. Life has somehow got in the way. Mundane shopping on a bank holiday, sweeping up the front path on a sunny Sunday, seeing aged relatives on any other day. It all takes you away from him, his presence. You don't want to spend any more time with him than you have to because there is nothing left to say.

You try. You suggest going out for the night. At least you can mingle with the crowd and pretend.

He doesn't want that. He wants you. On your own. You decide, finally, you just don't want him. It's done. You make something up to throw back at him when he asks, in tears, why you're leaving.

You know it's not the truth, but you say it, anyway. You tell him it has eaten away at you like a worm in an apple. You try to make it your fault and say that you know he is no longer happy with you.

When he asks again, *why?* you take a deep breath and respond.

I did what I did for you…for her. You tell him it's so he could go and be with this other woman. She's his boss and they spend a lot of time together, so it fits. You remember the late nights he's spent working away. You try to act jealous but know it's an excuse, a ready-made meal of distasteful lies that will leave a sour taste once you've gone. But you say it anyway. You know it's not real, but it's an excuse. A reason when you don't have a real one. All you want to do is to be alone, to be anywhere that he is not.

And then he asks. He asks you how you knew.

And you didn't. You made it up.

And you realise.

That is why you've lost that loving feeling.

You know that it was his fault after all.

Post-Mortem

I walk slowly from the car to the front of the house. My children wait up for me before they go to bed. They want a bedtime story. They want their mum.

Briefcase in one hand, keys in the other, I hesitate before I turn the lock. A soft dolly, a beanie baby, naked on the circular ebony table, is lying flat, looking out at me from the bay window. She wears nothing but a white felt hat.

Flash! I see her, eyelids half closed, mouth slightly open.

Flash! Scalpel line down her middle, intestines laying in a mess in the cold metal trough.

Flash! Head resisting the circular saw burning a rugged path inside her skull.

Flash! Jelly brain, expanded to mush, slopped into the formaldehyde bucket.

I blink. Dry eyes prepare me for the welcome I give to my son and daughters. Holding them tighter, squeezing until they catch their breath, I offer myself up to their warmth, their love.

The bedtime story, a ritual I perform to block out the sight. The ritual I do to keep things normal. A kiss for my baby, on her forehead, baby softness snuggles on my skin.

Flash! Liver, heart, kidneys, tiny organs sliced and taken to the microscope.

Flash! Splayed inert body, baby eight months, suffocated.

Flash! The frenulum torn, the hair pulled, the feet bruised underneath.

My children sleep, so I walk. I look up to the sky, out to the sea. I sit on a cold vandalised bench, with drizzle and mist a shroud to comfort me. I promise I will do my best. Find out the truth, for her, for me.

The passer-by walking her dog sees my tears and asks if she can help. It is a sign, people do care. Bad day on silver cold slab, but I don't say. The secrets in my head I try to keep hidden, protecting the children, the innocent, and keeping my own home safe. The post-mortems omnipresent, time and again, a harsh, brutal reminder every time I see a naked, soft- bodied dolly.

She is with me, always, the battered baby. She is one of many.

To Dance, To Dream

Anna Seigal loved, lived, and laughed. A lot. She also danced. She lived life like a Rorschach image, seeing what she wanted to see and ignoring the rest. She preferred others to see her that way too. Blithe perception, her mother called it, but it was just Anna's way.

'We need to get our heads together tonight, my dear,' said Bob as he handed her a steaming cup of strong tea, preparation for the chore ahead. 'Get together to go through this tax return.'

'Not tonight, Bob. It's light outside. I want to go dancing.' She smiled, without concern for his concerns. She wanted to dance.

'Dancing doesn't sort the paperwork, Anna. We need to have it ready. For tomorrow. And you promised.'

'Tomorrow, tomorrow. There is always tomorrow. And the day after, and the one after that.'

'No, my dear, there won't be a tomorrow if we don't take care of today.'

Anna frustrated him. She was always broke and he never knew what she spent their money on. Nothing tangible, he was sure, except for the odd things she brought into the house, often from the antique shop on the brow of the hill near the river. Things like the cut-glass salt and pepper shakers that she said she'd fallen in love with as she passed the shop window. Anna told him they glinted and smiled at her as the sun bounced off the worn edges and into her eye.

'They had my name on them,' she said, kissing him lightly on his cheek and sashaying away from his open arms, light skirts swinging, flimsy voice singing, 'I'm in the mood...'

Bloody Nolan Sisters. Bob's shoulders fell as he sat at the table scattered with invoices, cheque stubs, receipts, and paraphernalia he had garnered over the last twelve months. He should have known something was up when the bills stopped coming in, and credit card statements started disappearing. He hadn't noticed at first and then when he did, well, he could drive himself crazy, imagining things.

He guessed she was already in love when he met her but she saw something in him that nobody else did. She could see the Rorschach behind his brash, bulky, bear-like body. She touched something inside him which made him ping, made him more alive than ever. Whatever she did, wherever she went, it mattered not. He felt privileged she wanted to spend any time with him at all. He'd dreamt but never believed she'd say yes to his marriage proposal, but she did, and for that he was grateful. He would forgive her anything.

Their wedding in the bright open air was a beautiful affair and maybe that was all their relationship should have been. The memory of the day made it worth it – he in a conventional suit and she with flowers in hair, bare feet that made her laugh when the grass tickled, and a white gossamer dress that floated like feathers in the air. She chose the venue for their wedding, the place where her mother was buried in a humanist grave, held safe beneath the ground in a banana leaf coffin.

Anna kissed him lightly and smiled as she said, 'My dear bear, you see what you want to see,' as she pulled him along behind her and started to dance.

She may have been in love with him, or somebody else, or nobody at all. It never felt right to ask. He earned the money and gave her freedom to do as she liked and she always returned, but she was killing him.

Tonight, she came home past midnight, the hall clock done with chiming when he heard her key in the lock.

'Where have you been, Anna?' he asked.

'I told you, bear, see what you want to see. I've been dancing.' She took off her little flat shoes and tucked some strands of her blonde-white hair behind an ear. Her eyes sparkled like flying diamonds.

His heart melted a little and shrank as another piece faded away. 'I love you, Anna.'

She smiled and her eyes made him think of the spaniel he'd rescued from a frozen lake when he was a child. He wrapped his arms around her, and he felt her heart beating next to his and it melted away a little more. Another piece faded, gone.

'I know.' She kissed him, a light feather touch, like she'd evaporate if he held her too tight. 'Come to bed, my darling. Dance with me.'

And he did. But he didn't know how much longer he would be able to keep tune. She would certainly be the death of him.

Mrs Atkins

I think her name was Mrs Atkins, but I can't be sure. She said something that sounded like that. It doesn't matter because names are irrelevant, and I prefer not to put a name to them anyway as it makes it a bit more personal and I want to keep personal out of it. It never paid to dwell.

She looked the type, fat, frumpy, and maybe even divorced. She didn't wear a ring. She didn't look like a woman one would miss too much either, with her freakishly permed hair and black flat granny shoes. That was my plan, my best of ideas, someone who nobody would miss. I didn't want any nosy-osies poking around.

I got to know her with a bit of chit and some chat when she stood outside my flat waiting for the bus. I didn't want too much information because the more we talked, the more she could blab to somebody about me. Any new friends or acquaintances are often talked about and I didn't want to be anything significant. She'd met me, smiled and nodded but I had to keep it all low-key, just enough so she'd recognise me to say 'hi' and little else. I didn't want to know if she had kids, though I doubted it anyway, and I didn't want to know what she did for a living. I was only interested in passing the time of day at the bus stop until the number six rattled her away. A couple of months of a wave and a half-smile here and there would do it. It usually did.

I was biding my time, waiting for a wet day. This time of year, one never had to wait too long. Thursday, ten minutes past ten, freezing cold morning, and there she stood, waiting, stamping her flat, corn-obliging shoes and shaking her duffle coat head. Today was the day.

I left my ready and prepared flat, leaving the door on the latch, and I walked the few steps to where she shivered. I stood beside her and told her the news. 'Buses are all cancelled this morning. Something to do with the weather…floods…roads are blocked…or something like that.'

'What? Oh no.' Her mouth fell, and she stamped her feet some more.

She put me in mind of a truculent child, she did. 'You can make a call from my flat if you like,' I offered, pointing up to the top floor of the building behind her.

'Oh! Could I? Thank you,' she enthused and looked quite nice when she smiled like that. I had to stop the voice inside my head that told me to leave her alone.

It had been that easy. Not a bit of bother. I made tea, one sugar, plenty of milk. I could have guessed. She looked like the type. She needed to ring somebody, cancel an appointment or something, so I asked for the number, withholding my own first of course. Didn't want any of that 1471 business should anyone feel the need to check. Turned out she was ringing the nursing home that looked after her mother on account of the Alzheimer's. She said she hated the job of looking after her but there was no one else and she'd spent all her life looking after a twisted, possessive, manipulative woman she called 'Mum'. The day just got better and better. Who'd ever know? I hummed as I did the last-minute preparations in the bedroom while she spoke to whoever was on the other end of the line.

TAKING HER OUT was easy. I won't bore anyone with the details, but she didn't put up a fight. Then I really set to work. It would take all day and most of the night. I liked this bit best of all. I hated the beforehand, when they rambled on and on and I had to make small talk with a fistful of lies.

As she lay on my bed, waiting for me with her limbs outstretched in the shape of the Da Vinci Man, I decided to go through the plaid bag she'd had with her. Surprise, surprise, it wasn't full of granny clothes after all! I could get me a new wardrobe out of this little parcel of goodies. A little beige compact bag contained wonderful make-up of a brand I'd only ever heard of from the television adverts and expensive department stores; the type I never ventured into and certainly not the sort I could afford. Thick black mascara smelt of rich dark ink and various shades of lippy looked lustrous and expensive. I think I could appropriate those without too much difficulty. Black patent stilettos, size seven, a perfect fit! A long blonde straight wig, a couple of pairs of black fishnets, a rich ruby-red bodice, and a pair of glistening handcuffs. Wowzer! Who the hell was this broad? Were they her clothes? As if! I doubted it very much. But one never knows…

Time for a little attention to the body on the bed. I'd stapled black bin liners around the room a couple of days earlier, in anticipation of the full moon and pouring rain. I primed and prompted the chainsaw, brummmm, brummmm, brummmm…but first, I had to strip the little lady.

I unfastened the brown bear duffle coat. I thought I might keep that. I was rather partial to Paddington as a child and I'd always coveted one. The foster home didn't stretch to such things in the 1960s. I could have four outfits for the price of a duffle, and they had to last me a year or more, whether they fitted or not. Yes, I liked the coat. I'd keep that.

There were more surprises to come. The outfit behind the coat was rather sexy! So much for being frumpy! Or fat! She was certainly much younger than I'd imagined. I removed the low-cut bodice in black silk and tried it on. It fitted like Cinderella's shoe. Her brassiere revealed proud nipples, both pierced with gold hoops. I gave them a twang for good measure. As I stripped her further, the matching thong revealed a strip of delicate hair and surprise of all surprises – a dripping bloody red heart tattoo, stabbed through the middle with a dagger. How provocative, I thought, especially on the pubic bone.

The pain in my chest increased with the pounding that echoed behind my left eye. Danger signs bounced around in front of me and found a way to filter into my brain...*she was a hooker...a looker...a good-time girl...someone would miss her...look for her...want her...desire her...call her ...*

I'd mistaken her frumpiness and interpreted her look and distance for my own needs. Panic. Heart racing, light-headed, dry mouthed, clumsy-fingered. Must keep a clear head. Must keep calm. No one would know. The number, the telephone – who had she called? I'd only heard part of the conversation, uninterested, uncaring, believing what she'd said about an Alzheimic mother. Why would she have lied? Why to me? She had no reason. I wasn't a threat. No, not I. Not one that she'd guess, anyway. Or so I thought. Blasé. Too confident. Slap my wrists. There was a reason she'd lied. She had a secret and it was now discovered.

I had a thought. Therein lay a plan. Phew! It felt good as a cool sweat covered me in relief. If she did ply her trade, then it could be any one of a number of punters.

No one would suspect me, and as a local bod, I could confirm she regularly took the number six from outside my house but no, I hadn't seen for a while, come to think about it…

I continued and boy, once I'd stripped her completely, this girl looked like she done a few rounds in the gym. All that fat turned to muscle, little to waste. Where's that chain saw? Ah yes, brummmm, brummmmrrummmmmmrummm, raring and ready to go…strip jack naked and fiddle-de-dee. Ooh, I loved this bit. Split splat, an ounce of fat, a strip of loin and howsa about that. Bring in the stock pot and boil a bit of brine, add a stalk of celery and all is fine. Zippee-de do-dah, zippee-de-yay.

A few hours later it was time for meltdown. I had myself a pile of meat, some ready for freezing and the rest for stock. Throw in the salt and pepper, a few mushrooms, onions, and job's a good 'un.

The stock ready, all I had to add was the fillers, the button mushrooms, shallots, and meat, then a little later, a pot of cream. That'll do nicely thanks. The folk around here love a good feast in winter and I'm such a good neighbour. Especially when I wear my heels, fancy make-up, and a smile. They never suspect a thing about Miss D'arcy from number 3D, Pembrose Avenue, top-floor flat in the house behind the bus stop.

Fancy a stroganoff?

Bowl of Cherries

Previously published stories

Bowl of Cherries *First published Twisted Tongue Magazine 2010*

Look Me in the Eye *First published online Five Stop Story 2012 Highly commended*

On the Beach *First published Twisted Tongue Magazine (Vol13) 2010*

Tiny Little Feet *First published Against the Clock Anthology, 2006*

A Man Called Andy *Honourable Mention Multi Story 2012/ Longlisted Five Stop Story 2012*

A Way with the Kids *First Published Online Sentinal Literary Quarterly 2010, 3rd Place comp*

You Can't Change Time *First published Online Write Place 2011, 1st Place comp*

A Kind of Loving *First published Fygleaves Anthology 2006*

A Gypsy Woman Told My Mother *First published Right Eyed Deer –Body Parts Anthology 2010*

Playing with the House-Elves *First published Hastings Legend Writing Anthology 2009 2nd Place comp*

Hedgehogs, Green Bottles and Lilies *Writers & Artists Yearbook – shortlisted 2010 / Fylde Writer's Circle – shortlisted 2012*

Dancing with the Devil (1184) *First published online Five Stop Story 2012 Runner up*

Time Enough *First published online Write Invite 2010 1st place*

She Forgot All About Mikey *First published Global Short Story 2011 1ˢᵗ Place*

The Piano Man's Daughter *First Published online Five Stop Story 2012 Honourable mention*

Persuasion *First published online Secret Attic 2006*

Remembrance *Shortlisted 2010 JBWB,* *First published on Radio, Brighton Cow, 2011*

Haemorrhage *First Published online Cooldog 2010*

The Same Face *Shortlisted Get Writing 2012,* *First Published Writer's Forum magazine 2012*

That Loving Feeling *First Published Chuffed Buff Books 2012*

Post Mortem *First Published Twisted Tongue Magazine 2006*

Mrs Atkins *First Published online Global Short Story 2010*

Acknowledgements

I first started to write stories when I was five. Over the years I've written some strange stuff but when I sat down in 2004, I knew this time was for real. Being published was far from my mind at that point because I believed it could never happen. When I was five, I was told people like us read books, we didn't write them. I only knew that I wanted to write, and I meant it. I had no idea where it would take me.

Skip forward to 2020 and I've written thousands and thousands of words and met hundreds of writing-related wonderful people. I've had 155 short stories published and/or placed in competitions, under a variety of names. Harper Collins published my 'faction' book (under yet another pseudonym) and I have completed my first crime novel. It is currently out on submission.

Thank you to all my readers and supporters for helping me to believe that I could self-publish a collection of some of my short stories and thank you especially to all of those who have bought it, and an even bigger thank you to those who read it.

A writer always loves a reader.

Special thanks must go to my dear writing friend, Jo Derrick, as I could not have written majority of these stories without her encouragement, or her daily prompts. Great thanks to my editor, Emma Mitchell, who believed in me and showed me the error of my ways. If you want an editor, she comes highly recommended, not just by me, but by many great and fabulous writers. To my after-party Noir pals, you guys rock and don't forget – circle of trust!

To all of the supportive writing community, you're marvellous. In 2020 we have missed the festivals, the writing events, the launches, the conferences, and the gatherings. I can't wait to see you all again, somewhere safe, somewhere soon.

Effie x

Printed in Great Britain
by Amazon